NAOMI, DEBORAH, MICHAEL . . . AND A NEW LIFE

"Are you happy, Rosie?"

"No. No, I'm not happy. We should want to do everything to make the child happy. If she has two close friends that mean so much to her, why should we impose our will on her? Why?"

"My god," he sighed. "Isn't it going to be hard enough for people our age with two? Do we really need a third?"

She didn't answer. Her hands were pressed to her face.

"All right!" He jerked his chin at the director. "Who's the third?"

"By coincidence," said the director, "it's a little boy. Michael . . ."

"Rosie? You hear, the third one in the business deal is a boy. It won't be so bad, two girls and a boy. Is that all right with you?"

Rosie Howard was beaming.

Three Children
of the
Holocaust

Sol Chaneles

AVON
PUBLISHERS OF BARD, CAMELOT AND DISCUS BOOKS

THREE CHILDREN OF THE HOLOCAUST
is an original publication of Avon Books.

AVON BOOKS
A division of
The Hearst Corporation
959 Eighth Avenue
New York, New York 10019

First Avon Printing, September, 1974.
Third Printing

Printed in the U.S.A.

He tore the file in two, then in two again, letting the pieces fall haphazardly. A large envelope: snapshots—hospital wards, soldiers at the front lines, hills dotted with vineyards, olive groves, prisoners of war, a long column of them marching with their hands atop their heads, nurses, those pretty women with smiles and shapely figures, women from liberated countries, from occupied countries, civilian personnel of the armed forces, women in army uniforms: bedmates, companions for a fleeting night of sweetness. He smiled. With enough time I could dig a grave with my pecker. He crushed them with his hands. Another folder. Military medical reports. A large photograph of an interminable line of soldiers naked from the waist down, their trousers bunched against their boots. He laughed. VD inspection. A million bare peckers. The sun's energy harnessed in a small wrinkled bag: an atomic reaction, an eerie explosive light never before seen by man, shut up tight in a microscopic frantic, squiggling droplet of scum blindly driving, seeking out, penetrating its target. A million bare peckers, a hanging out of privacy. When the settlement check arrived he would travel to Italy, drink the waters, take mud baths, drink good brandy for a change, and get it up for the biggest and perhaps last lay of his lifetime. He sneered and tore the picture. So many are dead. Dead peckers. Ugh!

Chapter 1

THE BOOK OF NAOMI

How they got there can only be surmised. Nine years later a commission was set up by governmental decree to uncover the facts, conduct trials, print newspaper stories, erect a monument. But there were no records as such. After a few desultory hearings that produced little more than conflicting accounts by aging, therefore unreliable witnesses to the events, the commission disbanded, and the place became a cooperatively managed hotel for tourists. For some reason that no one could explain, the hotel specialized in omelettes filled with slivers of bittersweet chocolate.

The castle had forty rooms and there could have been as many as eight beds in each room. The teachers used some of the beds but mainly they were used by the children. How many there were will never be known. The commission tried to establish that the children slept two to a bed but even the old witnesses laughed at the number that notion would imply. More likely, there were three hundred, at most three hundred and fifty.

Borlice Castle is situated on one of the many grassy hills that roll gently down from the Slovenian highlands. It is a gray, fortresslike structure built of massive granite cubes. The employee-managers have had to hang bright red and vibrantly yellow draperies in the windows to make their castle hotel appear less forbidding. On rainy days the old building used to look so dreary that tourists didn't even bother to inquire whether rooms were available. Inside, Borlice Castle is more pleasant, inviting despite the fact that the stone walls wear only a cover of whitewash; the empty spaces between the stone moldings cry out for honey-colored wooden panels, but these are gone, burned as fuel years ago. The northern windows look out on the slow-moving, muddy waters of the Drava River as it makes its way southward, where, three hundred miles after it gurgles past the castle, it empties into the Danube.

People crossed the borders easily. But that was during the early days of the strange events. There was much talk about trouble but there was little of it. There were no newspapers. The radio played only music. Word about what was happening in the capital spread from mouth to mouth. Those who crossed the borders told strange tales about what was going on over on the other side. Most numerous among the visitors were children, especially in groups; the larger the group, the easier it was to cross. They were like sightseeing school children come to visit the Borlice granite quarry, renowned for myriad swirls of color that had appeared on the steep walls, and for the amazingly clear water that filled the quarry, water so clear that the colors could be seen as if the pit were empty.

The teachers gave assurances to the Borlice constabulary that the children would be properly fed and clothed. By prearrangement, the castle awaited them, the largest group that had ever crossed over at one time. Who had had the authorization? It was a recurring question during the commission meetings. Was it a rugged, heroic highlander worthy of a statue or at least a bronze tablet? Nobody came forth to claim the honor. Records were gone. Rumors about who it might have been led nowhere.

Many of the groups had come from the crowded orphanages and children's camps that had been hurriedly and reluctantly constructed in Graz, about seventy miles to the north. Every day trainloads of children and teachers would empty at Graz. When the old schoolhouse that had been converted into a warehouse for grain, and then hurriedly reconverted to a home, proved it could not contain the swelling numbers a section of the railroad station partitioned with boards and wire fences soon became a children's home. Children continued to pour into the city; none left. When talk began to spread that the opera house would have to be used, temporarily, to shelter them, groups began to leave. At night teachers were told, "Go. Take your children and go." They even received sacks of provisions and flashlights.

Some headed west, where they found fishermen who carried them to the islands off the coast. There they stayed until the autumn winds and rains came and many of the children developed fevers. Others headed south and waded across the shallow, muddy river, where farmers carried them by wagon to the empty Borlice Castle.

At Borlice Castle the most urgent problem that faced the teachers was dividing the children by the different languages they spoke. This turned out to be an impractical arrangement since many children spoke languages unknown to the teachers. They tried to divide the children according to age; this, too, proved impractical both because of language problems and the fact that in some age groups boys and girls resented being kept together. In any of the many languages spoken, there weren't enough books to go around.

For several weeks the children spent the days cheerfully sweeping and arranging the crowded rooms, washing and mending clothing, learning songs and dances to entertain the farmers and village shopkeepers who each day brought them baskets of food. Whining and complaining began on the day food deliveries stopped. In the evening of that day no one came from the village for the singing and dancing and the entertainments stopped completely. After a few weeks, the money the teachers had been able to carry in their undergarments when they left Graz, enabling them to buy a crate of scrawny chickens each week, was gone. At the beginning there were mouth-watering chicken stews; these gave way to soups with small chunks of chicken meat; then there were just thin, unsatisfying broths. When the singing and dancing classes disbanded because the children refused to participate, the teachers stopped smiling. The three hundred and fifty hungry mouths complained ceaselessly, there were constant fights, and as many younger children were punished for striking an older one as there were older ones who increasingly found the younger ones spiteful, mean, and bothersome. Older children laughed mockingly when the teachers told them that they had a moral responsibility to care for the younger, weaker ones.

Even the language, mathematics, and history classes stopped. Whole days would go by for many children with little more activity than sleep, games of tag through the many rooms of the castle, teasing, and fighting. Each day ten teachers accompanied by about ten children each trudged into the hills and villages in search for food. They left the castle just as the sun was breaking; some of the groups did not return until nightfall. At night, there was usually enough with everything combined in two huge kettles to make sure that everyone would be able to go to sleep, having had something to eat that day. After a while the complaints about hunger stopped; more time was spent sleeping and examining sores that began to appear on arms and legs. The children compared the size and coloration of their sores.

On some mornings as the foraging groups were about to set out, they found a number of villagers standing mute and patiently waiting for them on the flat, gravel-paved courtyard of the castle. Some leaned against the wall of the well that stood in the very center of the courtyard. They spoke angrily to the teachers. Hearing the heated conversation, some of the sick children or those whose turn it was to stay indoors peered from the windows or hid behind the massive wooden doors, listening and watching.

"There's no more food," a villager shouted.

"We've given everything."

"Now they beg."

"When we give nothing, they steal."

"They have become beggars and thieves."

"You must go away, or. . . ."

"Or?"

"Or we shall drive you away."

They were placated for the teachers gave them their own clothing: a sweater that had come from Paris, a plum-colored shawl from Budapest, scarves from Italy.

Also: watches and simple jewelry from Berlin, and birthday and anniversary gifts from husbands and wives, from parents and children, and delicate undergarments made in Milan, pocketknives from Switzerland. The gifts were accepted as restitution for what had been stolen.

During the day when the teachers cared for the sick ones and for other teachers on whose bodies large, angry sores had appeared, some of the children in bands of twos and threes violated the teachers' rule about not leaving the castle courtyard without an adult.

Two entered a small shop in a village, a shop that sold rancid cheese, chunks of cold salted mutton shanks, dried fish, and loaves of hard black bread as heavy and dry as stone. They pretended to argue and fight with each other, rolling on the clay floor, knocking over boxes and barrels of dried fish. The elderly shopkeeper took a cane to them and chased them onto the unpaved street. An awful commotion! He tried to separate them by striking their shoulders with the cane. During the mock battle, a third child ran into the shop and stole as much food as he could carry. When the shopkeeper became aware that he had been deceived, he brought his cane down on the children's backs with as much fury as he could muster from his old bones.

The teachers warned daily that the stealing was wrong and must stop. Late at night they met to discuss new punishments for the young wrongdoers. As they spoke, some shared crudely made cigarettes rolled from tobacco stolen by some of the older children and given to their favorite teachers. "Send them to bed without eating," was a refinement on prior punishments. This would invite further sickness; too many were already sick. One teacher who had been training for a doctorate in pedagogy, mused that they had achieved the Socratic vision of education: a school in which punishment had lost its moral persuasiveness and in which nature itself made its demands directly on the intellect. Another, who had been a student of philosophy, said: "Let us all convince ourselves that there are exquisite desserts served at the end of the meal. Those who violate our norms shall forgo, not the essential nourishment, but the unnecessary luxury."

"Marvelous idea! Consistent with this idea, and to make it democratic, we should be able to propose, each one in his turn, precisely which luxurious dessert should be the object of deprivation. Do you agree?"

"Agreed."

"Take away the Black Forest tart that is so close to my heart."

"Brandied cherries in champagne."

"Candied chestnuts topped with whipped cream."

"Blackberry strudel with powdered sugar."

"Walnut cake with sliced chocolate."

Like the children, some teachers slept clasped in one another's arms, for even on the warmest nights they felt chilled and a dampness was always in the air.

Now, when the children returned with stolen provisions, there was neither scolding or questioning. The meager loot was tossed into the pots; no child or teacher went to sleep without first eating at least something. When there were sermons against theft, the words and the tone sounded more like expressions of praise and gratitude than of disapproval. As long as there were articles of clothing or jewelry to redeem the stolen food, the farmers and villagers did not enforce their threat to evict them from Borlice Castle.

One day, in the middle of the season of the strong winds and heavy rain, one of the teachers ran into the castle and asked that everyone gather in the massive dining hall. He was breathless, and though chilled by the cold and the rain drenching his frayed garments, he smiled radiantly.

A new government! In celebration, everyone in the country was entitled to receive sufficient flour to make a full loaf of white bread. They would have the fine white bread that many had even had dreams about. Except for the sick ones, they all bundled in whatever clothes remained and marched, like scouts on a hike to the village. Some, mostly the younger ones, sang. If they were careful, the teachers cautioned, the miracle loaves might last a week. They marched alongside the river, held hands, and were not bothered by the wind or rain. The march took an hour; by that time, the governmental decree had been modified.

The new order decreed one loaf for every four persons. It didn't matter. They placed the sweet-smelling still-warm loaves under their clothing to keep them dry and marched back to the castle. As they marched farmers and villagers came from the hills with offers to trade for the warm white bread with dried fish, beans, olives, shriveled apples, blackened slabs of lamb, small sacks of raisins, even a few freshly slaughtered ducks. Under the imperfect shelter of swaying trees fierce bargaining commenced. Even the youngest children bargained with the villagers. When the march resumed, little was eaten from either the loaves or what they had been exchanged for. Not an olive nor a raisin was touched. Elaborate plans were made for the careful storage of the food and for more nourishing meals for a week or more. While the children did not understand what difference a new government made, the teachers were animated with hope. Most were convinced that matters would improve—soon they might return home.

From the other side of the river sounded a loud, noisy drone of airplanes. In the distance orange balls of fire and columns of black smoke billowed up into the gray, rainy sky. Explosions followed. The air and earth trembled. A bicyclist appeared, clumsily trying to ride over the muddy ruts in the road. He wore a long white cloth coat, heavy with rain, clinging to his shoulders. Tied to the back of the bicycle was a large metal box with bottles and packages taped to its sides.

"Let me pass. Quickly," he said breathlessly. The way was cleared.

"There are many wounded near the border."

"Wounded?" asked the teachers.

"An invasion has started."

"But the new government?"

"Finished. Let me pass." The mud sucked at the narrow bicycle tires.

One of the older boys looked at a teacher to whom he had given stolen tobacco. "No more bread?"

"We'll see."

As they entered the courtyard of Borlice Castle, the teachers gasped and covered the eyes of the smallest children with their hands. But there were too many eyes to hide from the scene.

The gravel pavement was covered with the blood-spattered bodies of young men. Blood gushed from wounds in their faces and arms. Standing over the bodies were soldiers holding pistols or rifles.

"You," shouted a soldier. "All of you! Dump them in the well. Fast! All of you."

One of the teachers went up to the soldier who had given the command. "This is our only drinking water."

He rammed the butt of his rifle into her breasts, catapulting her backward to the blood-drenched courtyard. A loaf of bread fell from her jacket and quickly turned red.

"Drink piss!" he snorted. "Hurry up. All of them. Into the well!"

Teachers and children alike dragged the limp young bodies to the well wall. It took several to lift the bleeding forms over the four-foot wall and push them down. Even the six-year-olds helped. They either placed the parcels of food they carried on the gravel pavement or the packages fell as they dragged the bodies to the center of the courtyard. The soldiers stomped the food with their muddy, reddened boots. Food, mud, and blood became indistinguishable. They stuffed the slaughtered ducks inside their leather jackets.

"Hey, you!" shouted a soldier to a five-year-old whose golden hair fell in wet ringlets onto her forehead. "What have you got under there?" He poked a bump under the child's sweater.

She removed the lump and held it forward in both hands. "It's white bread. It's good. It's because there is a new government. Here, eat some."

He kicked her hands and the white loaf flew into the air. It landed in a mound of dirty ooze, splitting, shattering. "Eat this," he bellowed and pushed her little face with its high cheekbones into the mud.

"Let's get the hell out of here," barked the soldier in command. A soldier grasped the buttocks of one of the teachers closest to the castle gate. "You're a sweetie," he said. "We'll be back for you and the other sweeties tonight and give you a good time." The courtyard was silent.

From the road came the muted sounds of mud sucking at heavy boots.

Today, the well wall has been covered with yellow-glazed tile and a bower of roses grows over the arch from which the water bucket and wheel used to hang. On sunny days, a dozen tables covered with checkered cloths are casually arranged around the bower and waitresses and waiters clatter over the gravel pavement carrying plum brandy, strong dark coffee, and omelettes filled with chocolate. On rainy days, the employee-managers quickly sweep away the rain, even as it falls into drain ditches that line the building walls. As a result the earth packed between the gravel rarely softens enough to ooze from the cracks. Many tourists come from many countries and many languages are spoken by the staff, not proficiently but in snatches sufficient to comprehend the tourists' wishes and to respond intelligently to them. The director of Borlice's Castle hotel studied at a hotel-management school and is able to greet tourists in English, French, Italian, German, Hungarian, Russian, Bulgarian, and Czech. On sunny days he glides graciously by the tables in the courtyard, exchanges some pleasantries, is offered and accepts a glass of plum brandy and by night he is tipsy and groans that he would rather have become a dentist. At the nightly management-committee meetings the waiters and waitresses and the others who do the gardening, cooking, and other chores make fun of him by mimicking the foreign-language greetings that he employs to make the tourists comfortable. When a comrade chambermaid found him naked and in bed with an English widow one morning, she laughed hysterically, not because of his nakedness or in mockery of the compromising situation in which he had been found with the English tourist, contrary to management rules, but because he had rebuked her when she appeared in the doorway—not in his native language, but English: "How do you dare?" For weeks his comrades taunted him in English with: "How do you dare?"

For a while no one moved. The rain swept down and the deep red faded. The oldest teacher, who could not have been more than twenty-three, said hoarsely: "All of us from here back to the gate, go to the kitchen and take all the pots there are. Go to the river and bring back water. Don't drink any of that water. It will make you sick. We will boil it first and take the mud from it. All of the rest of us, let us get down on our hands and knees and cover every part of the courtyard to pick up every bit of food that is left. We will clean it and have something nice to eat later when we are dry."

That night there was enough to eat. And enough was put aside to assure a meal the next night, but not a crumb of the white bread remained. Surprisingly, though, there were enough raisins for anyone who wanted some. The children went to bed silently, without complaints or whining or arguments. The youngest refused to go to their own beds and insisted on sleeping under the beds of the teachers. When all the children seemed asleep, the teachers moved quietly from room to room on the lower floor where there were a few empty bedrooms and removed loose boards from closets, shelves, furniture, even loose floorboards. They propped these against the front door, the two rear doors, and at least one board was wedged against every window on the lower floor; these would clatter to the floor and warn them if someone tried to open a window from the outside. They agreed to take turns staying awake and to warn the others if intruders appeared.

"And if they do come?" asked a teacher.

"We can't fight or protect ourselves."

"To be aware is sufficient," said the philosophy student. No one dared mention possible harm to the children, though it was on everyone's mind. As they were about to go to bed or take up the nocturnal watch, ten soldiers suddenly appeared. The doors flew open as if there were no locks, the boards that had been propped against them falling away as if they were only thin reeds, making scarcely a sound. The young men teachers moved toward the soldiers, defiance in their eyes and weakened bodies. Most were barely twenty years old. The soldiers smiled at them and almost effortlessly smashed pistol handles and rifle butts in their faces. They slumped to the floor and were kicked repeatedly in the stomach and groin. The terrified women looked on in horror, but made no sound to awaken the children.

"Let's get it over with," shouted the soldier in command. "Take your goddamn clothes off."

The women undressed obediently.

"Watch this, boys," said the soldier in command. "I'll teach you a few tricks with these sweeties." He tugged at the upper edge of his trousers and they fell down over his boots. The women's eyes avoided his exposed genitals.

"You first," he glowered, pointing to the nearest teacher. "Come on, boys, let's give it to them."

Before a single hand of the soldiers could touch the white, soft, trembling bodies, a score of young men dashed into the room, their faces distorted by anger and hatred; silver blades slashed swiftly into backs, throats, stomachs. The only sounds were death gurgles, bodies slumping to the floor, gasps from the teachers. Several young faces appeared behind suddenly lighted torches in the courtyard. The soldiers were dragged over the gravel to the well. The women ran out, unashamed of their nakedness, and helped throw the limp, uniformed corpses over the well wall. Children peered from windows on the upper floors. Some left their beds and went into the courtyard. The teeming rain washed the blood away quickly. The young men wore the plain clothes of villagers and farmers. On their heads they wore red-wool caps.

"Strip them," a young man ordered. "Everything. Clothes, boots. Everything. Before you push the bastards in."

Naked, the rain streaming down their young bodies, the women removed the soldiers' clothing.

"Go back," said the women to the children who had come into the courtyard. The children ignored the teachers' commands. They searched the pockets of the discarded uniforms. They found some of the precious articles given up weeks before to the villagers and farmers in exchange for food. Swiss pocketknives, pins, watches.

A young child with golden ringlets and high cheekbones clung to the naked thigh of a teacher as the woman pushed a body into the well.

A young man with a rifle slung over his shoulder pulled a two-wheeled cart into the courtyard. Guns, cartridge belts, boots, leather jackets, helmets, and bloodstained clothes were heaped into it. Wristwatches and trinkets were left on the gravel, however, for these would be useful in buying food. Like robots, the women helped heave the remaining bodies over the wall without emotion or revulsion. Some had never before seen the privates of a man. Some had never even sought such a view in a library medical book.

"Have you any food?" a young man with a red-wool cap asked a teacher, his eyes not yielding to the temptation to look lower than her own eyes.

"Enough for one day," she replied. "But we can share it."

"Good," he said.

A few of the teachers ran into the kitchen and, removing half of what remained in the cupboards there, brought it out to the young men.

Then the torches were snuffed out, and the score of men left as quickly and as silently as they had come. The children returned to their rooms. The women teachers dried themselves with their outer garments and donned their clothes again. Their young male colleagues were still on the floor, some unconscious, others writhing in agony. Through the night those who were unharmed attended to the others' injuries, wetting parched lips with cloths dipped in water, wiping away crusts of blood.

In the morning the sun shone briefly and the wind died down. A repugnant odor lay upon the corridors in the lower floor of the castle and the courtyard. Opening and closing windows would not make the smell go away. The odor clung even to the furniture and the teachers' clothing.

It did not take much time to prepare the morning meal of small flakes of dried fish and raisins boiled in discolored water from the river.

The adults conferred. They decided that immediately after the meal each teacher would lead twenty to twenty-five children from the castle and take whatever direction he or she felt would lead to safety. How to assign which children to which teacher? First, by the children's own preference, and, where there was no preference, by lot. After the meager meal, the plan was explained to the children. Half made their preferences known quickly and gathered in groups by the teachers they had chosen. For the remainder, page numbers were torn from a geography book and distributed to the children. Identical numbers were torn from another geography book and placed in a saucepan. The teacher took turns calling out numbers; as their numbers were called the children joined the proper group. Some hurriedly exchanged numbers when they wanted to be with another child. Some giggled as if playing a game that would be followed by other entertainment. "I hope I don't get the teacher with the space between his teeth," said a red-haired child.

There were kisses and hugs that seemed interminable, tears, and shouts of good-bye in many different languages.

"I never lived in a castle before," said one teacher to another with a constrained expression that spoke of wanting to say I hope to live to see you again.

"If all castles are as humid as this one, most kings must suffer from rheumatism," the second replied.

One group, made up mainly of younger children, walked until dusk, begging for food at farmhouses along the way. At last they came to a village by a railroad crossing, where they met a column of soldiers who seemed to be waiting for them. With the exception of a teacher and a golden-haired child who clung to her hand as if it were her own, the group was pushed inside a railroad car by the soldiers. The teacher and the clinging child with high cheekbones were pushed into a small wooden coal shed that stood by the side of the tracks. They were thrown to the splintered wooden floor and their clothes ripped from their bodies.

Outside the shed a soldier turned the volume of a radio as high as he could. Dance music blared. A tango. The soldiers laughed and shouted: "Hurry up you sons of bitches! We've got to get moving pretty soon."

Inside the train the children heard only the dance music. They listened in frightened silence—they had not heard music from a radio since the beginning of summer.

19

Shots rang out. The radio was turned off. The small child, her face grimy with coal dust, her clothing torn, was led from the shed and tossed into the railroad car. In the shed the teacher did not get up when the blonde child was grabbed and led to the train. A dark hole was in her face.

The train clattered north through the rain-swept mountains. There were many stops, cars were added, and many additional passengers got on. There was much shouting and crying. The journey lasted three weeks.

Twice a day food was thrown into the car. One at a time the children were allowed to jump down and relieve themselves in the space between the tracks. They spent most of their time sleeping or looking blankly ahead. Some gazed out of the windows at the fields or forests but without curiosity, without seeing. The child with the blonde ringlets could not see enough. First awake, last to sleep, most of the time she pressed her face to the dirty window: lines of hanging laundry, soldiers, farm animals, wagons and horses, airplanes, houses, villages, late autumn flowers, telephone poles and wires, geese, people working in the fields. There was a constant feeling of nausea while the train was in motion as well as when it stopped and soldiers threw in crusts of bread daubed with unpleasant-smelling margarine and unpeeled boiled potatoes. At many stops, the blonde child noticed passengers who leaped onto the cars, abandoning their suitcases on the platforms. These were snatched by young people who ran away with them. As the train moved slowly around a long curve she saw that many cars had been added. They were all going home. Where would so many people stay? When the child felt like vomiting she pressed her face hard against the window so it began to hurt.

On arriving at Auschwitz, an older woman caressed her golden curls before shaving them. She kissed the little, pointed cheeks. "It'll grow back," she said. She cut away the hair, almost to the scalp, slowly, with fond words to calm the child. The caresses were sincere as she looked into the frightened blue eyes.

"What is your name, little child?"

"Child," the girl said, mimicking the woman's word. She did not understand the language.

"I'm the cook for this section and you will be my little helper. I shall teach you to be a great cook. You shall see what we can do with a turnip and potato."

She sat the child on her lap. The hair was shaved. The head was covered with a pale-yellow fuzz like a field of corn stubble.

"I'm going to call you Naomi. That's my daughter's name. She's far away. I won't see her for a long time. Come, Naomi, I'm going to teach you how we can make a beautiful stuffed roast goose from a turnip. And if I catch you eating even one little peel I'm going to spank your bottom so hard that you won't be able to sit on the lovely silk cushions in the parlor."

The child smiled, a smile of weary relief. For a moment she felt like falling asleep on the woman's lap, cradled by the woman's arms.

"You call me Auntie Felicia," the woman said.

"Auntie Felicia," the child repeated, understanding.

"Yes, dear Naomi," she said, "your auntie."

Chapter 2

THE BOOK OF DEBORAH

There was no mailman in Lizaky. It was too small a place to have one of its own. Only ten families lived there aside from the few gypsies camped beside the stream that ran from the hills above Lizaky a few miles to the point where it ended in the Kacak River. The few letters and parcels that came to Lizaky were delivered by a mailman who traveled by bicycle on the hard dirt road, alongside the hop fields, the few miles from Lidice. When it rained or snowed there was no delivery at all.

Agricultural records tell the little there is to know about the village: thirty-six milch cows (including heifers), six dray horses, close to a hundred chickens, fifteen bristly hogs, one cat, seven dogs, and a few geese. Lizaky's hop production amounted to eight hundred bushels a year; tough apricots fit only for jam totaled half that amount. The seven dogs wandered through the narrow alleys between the mud and straw-thatched cottages; everyone fed them scraps; they were claimed by no one.

The largest building in Lizaky was the shed in which hops were stored until trucks came from Plzen to pick them up; it was about fifteen yards long and twenty feet wide, and covered with a rust-streaked corrugated-iron roof. The village had no church and no church records, no notary, no village clerk, no school or school records, and, while some of Lizaky's children walked the few miles to the schoolhouse at Lidice, no one knew for sure how many went to school or were even required to do so. Year in and year out there was always an infant nursing at its mother's breast as she sat in the cool shadow of a barren plum tree; some children always seemed to be chasing the geese that fluttered their wings wildly as if recalling an instinct of flight, then ran off honking to the gypsy camp. Year in and year out there always seemed to be boys and girls old enough to hide in the sheaves of hops where they spent part of the night kissing and giggling, and there always seemed to be a scowling young farm worker who threw stones or leaves at the gypsy's wagon, or sometimes leaves wrapped around chicken droppings. In summer and during holidays, a writer or a teacher came to Lizaky to spend a week drinking milk fresh from the cows, eating freshly laid eggs, and nibbling at carrots pulled from the soil. He waded in the stream, napped in the hop fields, read newspapers and books in the shaded alleys between the cottages.

At different times of the year the number of Lizaky's children increased temporarily by one or two for a few days, sometimes for as long as a month. A family from the capital drove up to one of the cottages, conversed, drank milk, ate a few rye-seed cookies, deposited a child and suitcase, and departed. The child sometimes was from a family about to go on a business trip and was being left in the care of distant farm cousins. Sometimes the child was one who behaved badly in the school just off Wencislas Place and it was thought that to learn the ardors of simple country life would cure the child of meanness. Such a family was usually of modest circumstances; misbehaving children of rich families were sent to youth hostels and private schools in the Tatra Mountains or to the youth camps of Karlo Vary, where children all wore white shirts and pants or skirts. Families with limited resources sent their children to the countryside only twenty miles from the capital. The farmers did not haggle over prices and unlike the chic resort places, they did not ask embarrassing questions—Where are you from? We have to check your papers. We need this registration form completed showing your occupation. Your passport, please. Are you a damned foreigner? Are you a degenerate Jew?

Nobody hurried in Lizaky, but no one had time to ask questions about matters that didn't concern them, either. In Lizaky they read no newspapers, did not listen to the radio, were unconcerned about the political activities in the capital. Occasional outbursts of anger and resentment were directed at the gypsies who lived under a tent attached to the roof of their wagon, the wagon seeming almost on the verge of tipping over and falling into the stream that ended in the Kacak River.

On a day, early in June when all the hop vines were capped with bunches of pale yellow flowers, a column of black smoke curled up from the direction of Lidice. The smoke curled upward from mid-morning and continued until the moon rose and the hop fields were a vast gauze curtain of yellow. By morning the column of smoke had gone, but a wind blew from the nearby town, carrying a dreadful stench. The cows nudged each other testily on the way to the milking sheds. The pigs grunted moodily and turned away from the swill tubs. Chickens and geese jerked their heads nervously and paid no mind to Lizaky's only cat who wandered nervously among them. Only the dogs seemed undisturbed; wherever there was shade they slept and occasionally twitched an ear or growled to ward off flies.

The mailman rode slowly into the wide space between Lizaky's cottages.

"Why does it smell so bad?"

"What was burning in Lidice?"

A woman with an infant at her breast came up to him. An old man with a cane hobbled beside his bicycle. Some of the farmers who had been tending the vines of hops ran from the fields. Lizaky's children surrounded him, their eyes wide with curiosity.

He cleared his throat and bit at the gray ends of his thick mustache: "They say some young boys killed the governor who was living in Hradacny Palace. They say that the boys who did it went to hide in Lidice. They say that the people of Lidice must pay a price. They say that everything in Lidice shall be burned to the ground. They

24

say that all the children of Lidice have been sent far away and all the women, too. All the houses have been burned down, all the barns, all the trees, all the animals."

"And the men?"

"What about the men?"

"The men of Lidice?"

"Shot!"

"Dead?" asked the old man with the cane.

"All dead."

"All?"

"All?"

"Three hundred shot. All dead."

The children scrambled away shouting: "All dead. All dead." The shouts of a merry game, a new game. They ran into the yellow-flowered fields laughing gaily, disappearing in the fragrant furze. The older ones ran to the hillock overlooking the gypsy camp and threw stones at the wagon.

A little more than two weeks later several military trucks clattered on the hard, dry roads leading into the wide space between Lizaky's cottages. A squad of soldiers descended. They wore black uniforms and had rifles slung over their shoulders; their black boots gleamed. It took perhaps an hour to bring all of Lizaky's population into the wide space. How many? No one knows. The geese honked angrily at the men in black uniforms. There were four trucks, their roofs were rib cages covered with green canvas. The women and the tiniest children were lifted and thrown into the first truck. Boys over fourteen and men were struck on the head with foot-long truncheons and thrown into the second. The gypsies and hogs were thrown into the third. In the last truck the soldiers threw children between four and thirteen.

The roundup was over. The trucks drove off. Only two people remained in Lizaky: a child of eight who was holding the hand of an elderly woman. They stood watching clouds of dust curl up against the back of the last truck as it grew smaller and smaller. The dust settled. They stared.

In the truck with the youngest ones there was uncontrollable laughter whenever the wheels struck a rut and they jolted from the floor. The very youngest cried until they dozed off. An hour or so after it had left Lizaky the truck stopped. Puzzled, reddened eyes searched for understanding. Were they at their destination? Would they join those in the other trucks. One of the older boys peered through a seam in the green canvas: an empty road. No other trucks. No sign of the others. Some of them thought: Are father and mother waiting? Would there be a pot of fresh milk on the kitchen table with a thin slice of dark bread and a scoop of apricot jam? A soldier pulled aside the rear canvas flap and deftly hopped inside the truck. Grabbing the three- and four-year-olds by the hand or foot or whatever came first into his reach he flung them, still crying, to the side of the road. One, two, three, four, five, like sacks of coal, like bushels of dry leaves. One of them cried: "Mama! I didn't do anything wrong."

"Who else?" he said, grimacing. "Any other crybabies?" Some heads shook in reply. Eyes were fixed on the black uniform. He leaped to the road, fastened the flaps to close out the bright sunshine. The truck lumbered on.

"You want to see magic?" said an eleven-year-old boy to the plump, dark-skinned girl seated beside him. Her trembling fingers were toying with the frayed ends of her skirt. She was five or six, her dark hair cut short, bangs on her forehead. She nodded.

"My grandfather showed me," he exclaimed proudly. He removed a large silver coin from his trouser pocket. It was not a coin in current usage; it was from another age, another kingdom. It could have been a souvenir celebrating the inauguration of a provincial administrator; it could have been the decoration from the front of an expensive box of chocolates or candied fruit.

He placed the coin between his thumb and forefinger and, with a slight flick of the wrist, the coin vanished as if plucked from his hand by an extra-worldly power.

His companion smiled. A few other children looked on indifferently.

"Now watch," he said as the coin reappeared between his fingertips. The silver disc seemed balanced on the tip of the forefinger. "Abracadabra," he intoned in a shrill falsetto, "what we see is not real, what is real we cannot see!" For a fleeting instant, the coin seemed suspended in air, then it vanished.

The dark-eyed girl giggled.

He showed his palms. Empty.

The prestidigitation was repeated several times and the magic formula incanted. Soon, even his companion looked away, no longer interested. The rumble of the vehicle's engine drowned out the whispers and whimpers.

The truck stopped. The canvas flap opened. The horizon was a layer of russet. Dinnertime. Dogs yapped now by the gypsy camp, expecting a fire to be lighted under a deep copper cauldron. Cows stretched their thick necks over the fence to tear at the hop vines. A nervous cackling came from the shed, where chickens fought for a warm roost.

"Out!" the men in black shirts shouted. They pulled out the first ones closest to the back flaps of the truck. One, two, three, four, five, six, maybe more. Teeth were biting fingers; the youngsters lay on the side of the road where they had been thrown. They were silent. Large eyes looked for understanding. The sun was gone. Darkness pulsed.

"These?" a soldier asked.

"No," was the reply. "Let's get back in."

The motor ground and the truck lurched forward.

Inside the truck there was more room now. The children stretched out as if preparing for bed.

"Here," said the boy, placing the coin in the plump hand of the dark-eyed girl. "You keep it. You know the magic words?"

"Abracadabra." Her voice imitated his falsetto.

"That's right. My grandfather says that girls are only good for tending geese and that they don't know better. Do you think so?"

She shrugged and in the darkness he sensed the response against his shoulders. She made a fist around the coin and could feel moisture form in her palm.

It was cold in the back of the truck. Way past dinnertime—they were never up so late without dinner.

The truck stopped. Two soldiers leaped into the back of the truck. Shrieks of pain as their boots landed on the small bodies. Kicks. Shoves. The children fell onto the hard road. A crackling noise in the stillness, a white glow surrounding the muzzle of a pistol, a misty halo. Another sound like the abrupt snap of a dry branch, then another and another. A series of flashes. The dark-skinned child was last. She was kicked into a rut the size of a cradle. She saw the flash and heard the brittle crack, then a screech beside her, the sound of a cork tightening in a barrel of vinegar. She remained silent, motionless, even when the truck's engine gargled hoarsely and the small rear lights gradually disappeared. The journey from Lizaky was over: no lights, no familiar faces, no sounds, nothing moved in the darkness. Exhausted, she slept.

When she woke she saw before her the immense trees of the Bohemian forest. A dense fog enveloped the road; tendrils wrapped about tree trunks. She smelled no odor of boiling coffee. Birds chirped. She saw brown wings flitting between the branches, darting in and out of the fog. She opened her palm and saw the silver coin. She tied it to a torn end of her skirt in the way her mother had taught her to carry small coins. A double wrap, then a knot.

She walked along the rutted road and watched her shadow shimmer playfully in the fog. The sun warmed; glistening beads of dew hung from the leaves and spider threads swayed in the fog and changed colors. Very soon she came to a mound on the road. Was someone asleep? Clothing splattered red. The boy beside her in the truck. His eyes and mouth were open. Flies crawled on his tongue. She shook his shoulder.

"Hey. Come on. We'll go back."

No response. The shaking merely turned the twisted body further on its back.

"Abracadabra," she said in a shrill voice as she touched the coin tied in her skirt. No response.

The fog lifted. She continued along the road. She came to a second, a third, a fourth young body—some with arms and legs spread, some hunched in an awkward lump. None moved. She walked on. She felt the knot of her skirt hitting against her knee. The day became warmer. A large brown farmhouse showed from the corner of a sizable clearing on one side of the road: a steep roof with slabs of gray slate. In the meadow a chestnut horse tugged the braces of a plow; the girl saw furrows of rich, dark earth. A tall, husky man, bare to the waist, snapped the reins.

"Heu! Heu! You bastard, move!"

The pungent odor of animal manure enveloped the meadow. The girl stood at the edge of the field, a finger in her mouth. The horse's ears jerked up and forward. A short whinny. The muscular beast balked at the traces. The farmer stopped, gathered a double loop of rein, and cracked them onto the horse's flank. The animal's pointed ears stood erect, twitching, the nostrils flared. The farmer turned and saw a gray dress, a fringe of black hair, dark plump legs.

"What the hell is this?" he muttered.

He tied the reins to the one of the forked handles of the plow and walked slowly with large strides across the furrows.

"Who the hell are you?"

She looked up at him with pleading eyes. He spoke a strange language.

"A witch from the forest?"

No reply. No understanding.

"Are you lost?"

Nothing.

"You don't hear? You don't have a tongue in your head?"

Silence.

"Your name?" he said in another language. "What's your name?"

"Choux-choux," came a trembly voice.

"Choux-choux," he mimicked and rocked with laughter.

"Hungry?" he asked in the child's language.

She nodded.

"Come." He lifted her into his bare, chunky arms. He trod in the deep furrows toward the farmhouse.

He bellowed a woman's name even before he entered the low-ceilinged kitchen. A pot of coffee stood on the black, iron stove, alongside a pan of scalded milk. Familiar smells.

He shouted the name again. "Here," he said in a deep, booming voice, "I brought you a sack of potatoes."

"Potatoes?" said the woman entering the kitchen. "My

god!" She saw a child clinging to her husband's thick neck. "Whose child?"

"Who the hell knows? She's hungry. Feed her. She's from the other side of the forest. Understands only that language. Feed her, for crying out loud, instead of looking like a scared hen. See how her mouth waters at the sight of the pan of milk, like a pregnant cat."

They sat her on a wooden bench and watched as she devoured everything that was set before her. Crusts of bread soaked in the warm milk, a slice of sausage, a chunk of ham dipped in goose grease.

"We can't keep her here," said the woman.

"Why not?"

"In the village they'll find out we're keeping a foreign child. We'll be in hot water."

He nodded. "More milk?" he said to the child in her own language. She smiled. "Give her more," he commanded his wife. "We'll keep her for a few days. Then we'll do something."

"Suppose she's Jewish? Then you know what will happen to us?"

"Are you crazy? How can anyone tell if she's Jewish? She's a child. Her name is Choux-Choux."

Hearing her name, the child looked at them appreciatively.

Everything was familiar. Stove, dishes, bread, milk, the smell of coffee, grownups who gave things that were good.

"That's a crazy name, anyhow," he said. "Let's call her the same as you—Helga. Helga. You, fat little wandering witch from the forest, you, you're Helga."

It was a game. The child beamed. She repeated her new name.

"She is smart," the farmer said. "Wash her up. I'm going back to that bastard horse." He clambered out, his heavy shoes striking the wide, gleaming floorboards.

The woman could not scrub away the blue streaks on the child's arms and legs which at first she thought were dirt. She removed the dress and undergarments and found the welts and purple swellings. "My god, little child! You are so banged up it doesn't even hurt."

Little Helga was placed in the conjugal bed and warm,

dampened towels placed on the largest bruises. Then she was covered with a puffed-up goosedown quilt so that she was only a dark speck on the wide bed. In a few seconds her eyelids closed and she slept.

When neighbors visited, the child was hidden in a linen closet. It was warm and comfortable there. It was a game that she played eagerly.

The few days stretched into weeks, the weeks into months. The fields were harvested. In the sheds stood sacks of potatoes, turnips, and giant carrots all ready to be loaded onto a wagon and taken to the central market in town. The two Helgas sat beside each other on a bench in one of the sheds and shelled beans. The pods would be dried, shredded, and fed to the horse. They chopped cabbages and tossed the tough slivers into a huge wooden barrel that had a sour smell. The child had learned the farm couple's language. The woman no longer nagged her husband to send the child away. All summer long not a single patrol came to the farm. Then, as the days grew shorter, the woman saw a green car moving between the far side of the meadow and the wall of forest. "Hurry, to the closet and be very still," she told the child. "Quick." She called to her husband, who was loading sacks of produce onto an unhitched wagon on the far side of the shed. The car rounded the curve that led onto the farmhouse driveway.

The woman behaved as if it were a casual visit. One man in uniform came into the house. The driver and two others walked about the edges of the field and into the sheds.

A pitcher of cool beer, a plate with slices of sausage, cheese, and bread. The soldier accepted the hospitality with thanks. He commented that it seemed winter would be coming earlier this year. Probably much snow. Yes, and thanks to farmers like them, there would be no food shortages in the cities or for their heroic troops. Soon, he mused, everything would be back to normal. He, now an officer and formerly an accountant from a well-established firm from Dortmund, would probably take up farming then because, as a result of having been stationed in this area for almost three years, he loved farm life. With a wink, he suggested that he even fancied a young lady whose family they probably didn't know.

Neither the farmer or his wife spoke during his monologue. They did not betray their concern that the child might be discovered. She had performed well so many times during the past months.

A soldier entered the kitchen and reported that everything appeared correct; the men awaited his instructions.

"Excellent," said the officer. "Everything seems fine. I should, of course, look about your rooms. . . ."

"Of course," said the farmer with a slight bow. "Let me show you the way."

The officer smiled. He waved the thought away.

"No need. Just routine. You see, there has been a movement of illegal aliens in the region. Jews, political criminals, gypsies, spies, and god knows what other trash. Destructive elements! Some are hidden on our farms."

"Bastards," the farmer swore. "That's awful."

"Indeed. Some of our farmers are even taking bribes from these criminal elements. But you know, my dear farmer, they will be punished when we catch them. Prison. Labor camps in Poland. Harboring criminals is a very serious matter. They might even. . . ."

"Yes?" the farmer asked.

The officer slapped the leather pistol holster looped to his belt. "This."

"Dreadful," the woman said with a shudder.

"Unfortunately. But we shall have to have regular patrols. Thank you for your hospitality. Your own sausage?"

"Yes," answered the farmer.

"Delicious!" He saluted briskly and walked to the car. The shadow of the vehicle raced against the wall of trees by the forest road.

When little Helga grew into womanhood she forgot, as most children do, how the forest looked at sunset on the eve of the autumn season. Those who love forests but live at a considerable distance from them travel whenever possible to visit, to fill their lungs with a tingling freshness, to excite, at the same time to soothe, their eyes with the miraculous transformation of plain green leaves into a dizzying spectacle of many colors. Few of those who knew forests as small children can recall the brooding silences, the sudden rasping sighs, the blaring amplification of rain slashing the rotting forest floor. Nor do they seem to remember the hollow scratching of small animals on the ice, the maniacal, frenzied dance of the fog among the trees, the ticking away of insects at fallen seeds.

"Now!" the farmer's wife hissed, slamming a callused fist on the table. "Are you going to do something?"

"In a few days."

"Are you out of your mind?" Her eyes bulged. "You want prison? You want Poland?"

"All right. Dress her. Dress her warm. Fix a package of something for her to eat."

He brought the chestnut horse from the meadow and hitched it to the wagon laden with sacks of vegetables. His wife brought Helga out. The child wore two sweaters that the woman had knitted for her during the summer, knee-length stockings, and a pair of heavy brown shoes the woman had bought in the market as a birthday gift, she had said, for a niece.

"Good-bye child," she said softly to the child, hugging her, kissing her cheeks many times.

"You don't like me? I'm not a good girl?"

"Sure, you're good," she answered as she tucked the child's long stockings into the edge of an undergarment. "But you have to go someplace else. You don't belong here."

He lifted the child onto the wagon and arranged the heavy sacks so that she was concealed, but not uncomfortable. Another game. She asked no questions. Through a space between the sacks, the woman handed her a cloth parcel that held pieces of sausage and cheese. The man looked at her one last time before he sealed the narrow space. "What are you, my child: a spy, a political criminal, a gypsy, a Jew?"

A little hand reached out from between the sacks with a silver coin in the palm. "For you," she said. "For you, from me. I'm little Helga."

He took the coin and held the small, plump hand in his own for a moment.

"Heu!" he snorted to the horse. *"Heu,* you goddamn bastard, get moving."

It was dark. On the outskirts of the village he lowered himself from the wagon, angrily pushed the sacks aside, and took the girl into his arms. He looked at her and without a word set her on the paved road. He climbed back into the wagon, snapped the reins against the horse's back, and rode on.

Little Helga was picked up by the driver of the next passing wagon and turned over to the authorities who put her in an orphanage. From there she was taken, along with many other children her own age, to a very clean clinic operated by a pharmaceutical company. Each day the children received medicine and blood was drawn from their arms or necks. For a few weeks after being given some orange tablets to swallow Helga vomited constantly and was confined to bed. She became very thin. When the vomiting stopped and her appetite returned, she grew plump again and the dark color of her skin returned. One day, the men and women who gave the children medicine and took blood from them came into the dormitory and, with cheerful smiles, told them that they were transferred to a beautiful school with good food and many toys to play with.

The five hundred children from the clinic went by train to a camp at Mathausen. By the time they arrived, all either vomited or bled from the mouth. In the single, large building where they lived with only straw on the floor, the guards who tossed their meals of vegetable peels at them pinched their own noses to shut out the stench of vomit, diarrhea, and festering sores. There was no school, no teachers, and there were no toys. Because the children were ill and kept indoors and because the building's only windows looked out on other barracks and a bleak sky filled with snow clouds, they were indifferent to their surroundings and rarely talked to each other.

A nurse in a starched white uniform appeared each morning and evening and distributed medicine; no blood was drawn. Sometimes a guard spread fresh straw on the wet, filthy bedding; sometimes several guards entered and handed each child a cup of hot liquid. From time to time a guard found lifeless bodies in the straw and they were carried out by the feet and thrown in a cart. Sometimes a child refused the nurse's medicine or spit it up. When this occurred, the nurse said, in a voice loud enough for all to hear, "Bad child. Bad boys and girls. If you don't take your medicine you will be taken away."

One day the camp administrators received a letter from the capital. It ordered orphaned children below the age of ten, and over the age of four, prepared for future transfer to schools and subsequent education toward full citizenship. Immediately the filth was removed, the dormitory painted in bright, cheerful colors; the administrators installed beds and mattresses and nourishing well-prepared food was brought in three times a day. The children talked to one another and went frequently to the window, curious to see the outside. The guards delivered toys, and by the end of the month the one hundred and eighty remaining children seemed healthy and playful. Then another letter arrived from the capital. This new letter ordered further preparation of children for citizenship halted; moreover, children were ordered not to be kept even for one day at the camp in Mathausen.

Early one morning a few days later, the guards told the children to leave the dormitory and run to a train that waited for them. The journey took a week; it was a trip without food and without heat. Some of the children tried to talk, but found that the children they chose to talk to did not understand them. Others tried to play, but tired after a few minutes. When they arrived at Auschwitz, only forty still lived, little Helga among them.

Chapter 3

THE BOOK OF MICHAEL

A cloudless, sunny day filled with a somber rumor. Grim-faced Paris policemen spread it, as usual, but unlike yesterday's hint of dire consequences, this one, they felt quite certain, was real. Act accordingly, they warned, their gruff voices urgent. Unlike most of the rumors passed about, and squeezed dry by mid-morning over a small brown cup of ersatz coffee, this one grew. Details accumulated—so specific, so consistent, that this rumor had the semblance of unassailable truth. The densely crowded streets of the XIth arrondissement picked it up, passed it from mouth to mouth, to be repeated even by lips that pooh-poohed the everyday, early morning rumors.

It seemed, from the beginning, a certainty: there would be a roundup of sixty-five hundred undesirables. Foreigners, deserters, released prisoners of war, unregistered prostitutes, foreign women who had given birth to children fathered by Aryans, people suffering from terminal illnesses, the seriously defective, and especially Jews.

A policeman walking his beat stopped mechanically before, say, the cobblestoned entrance of a grime-blackened apartment house, casually wiped the sweat from the red-silk lining of his hard, round cap, and hissed between his teeth: "For anyone whose papers aren't in order, it's the end. They had better beat it, fast. Pass the word."

By eleven o'clock, when most rumors were stale and

forgotten, panic swept the quarter. On some streets rumor said only men would be rounded up. On other streets, rumor said no room of any building would remain unsearched. In the Popincourt sector, one of the most thickly populated in the city, the people despaired. Many elderly people there who had until this nineteenth day of the month withstood their fear with alertness and calm, now, as the day drew toward noon, became wretchedly senile, drooling, babbling incoherently, soiling their clothes, wandering aimlessly in the crowded streets.

At least once a day during the past weeks the neighborhood had experienced vicious assaults by attacking bands of young hoodlums. Small children were beaten with sticks and chains. Older people were robbed of their meager possessions. Worst were the raids in their rooms. Furniture splintered, canaries released from their cages, photographs of relatives torn, and official papers shredded and thrown about dark rooms like confetti amid hoots of derisive glee. The youthful hoodlums carried off anything of value, shouting: "France for the French!" On this day, the bands seemed more numerous, the thievery, beatings, and taunts more savage.

By dusk, thousands of residents in the XIth arrondissement trembled, waiting for the horrible truth to be visited on them. Many women whose husbands had already been deported waited for darkness. Then they grasped their children firmly by the hands and crossed the city through darkened streets and alleyways and sought refuge in the home of a friend or relative as a first step in a pilgrimage to some unknown, desperately hoped-for haven. A few, very old, very tired people put a silver coin in the gas meter, turned on the brass spigot, and placed their heads in the oven. Others drank large quantities of disinfectant and went to sleep. Mothers with newborn infants wrapped them in cotton blankets and placed them at the entrance places of public buildings.

On the morning of August twentieth the hollow-cheeked, gray-haired concierge of the National Home for the Deaf and Dumb, 254 rue Saint Jacques, finished the last crumb of the wedge of coarse, straw-colored bread dipped into a bowl of boiled milk, slipped her feet into her battered felt slippers, and as was her custom took a broom of green briar twigs and swept the steps in front of the grimy building. With luck a neighbor might stop and re-hash yesterday's rumors. She was not surprised to see the small, tightly wrapped bundle from which a wisp of hair protruded.

"Another little one!" she exclaimed, smacking her lips. "That makes six this week. If only there were enough milk. Enough room."

Among the scores of children, especially the older ones, many were genuinely deaf and dumb. Increasingly children arrived who were neither. Staff members did not pretend that they harbored children without identification. They made no distinction as to origin. The folders showed nothing that reflected adversely on the child's citizenship; all were French. No one claimed them? How could valid claim be established? None of the staff believed in the miracle of parents and children one day uniting. They prepared useful French citizens. They were not bothered by government clerks or committees of inquiry. The police regularly delivered their quota of ration coupons, never questioned how many more mouths there were this week compared to last month. No investigations. No suspicions. The arrangements seemed safe enough.

On August twenty-first the worst of the rumors came to pass. Speculation became fact. Hoodlums ransacked apartments as they were emptied or abandoned and from nowhere and everywhere swarms of the homeless appeared and filled them up again. The policemen pushed some into vans as they were told to and when they could they whispered: "Get out of here, fast. Don't run. Beat it." It is said, it is estimated, that on that day approximately six to eight thousand from the XIth arrondissement were rounded up, squeezed into trucks, and transported to Drancy. However, as the history books and commissions later put it, the plain truth was that eventually no one knew how many were taken. They were too occupied to count. On rue Saint Jacques, in the National Home for the Deaf and Dumb, they took every child who uttered a sound, including all the wailing infants.

The day remained cloudless. Word spread to the other

arrondissements—only the XIth was targeted. According to the afternoon newspapers, an abundant supply of fish was expected for the last week of summer vacation, the price of used cars declined, gasoline costs soared, students who failed their school examinations in July sat in the parks and studied, a certain lightness in the air. A weight lifted from their part of the city.

Drancy had been a camp for French prisoners of war. They were all sent away, many demobilized. It was a landscape that felt sorry for itself. With few trees there were scarcely any birds whose flight broke the monotonous lines of sky and fields. Orderly roads divided the land as far as the eye could see. Skimpy brush without flowers, a thin forest, trees like bean poles dressed with meager, lifeless foliage. Even worms seemed to avoid the drabness of the region, for the crops of cabbages and beets rarely sufficed to bring the kind of money commensurate with the acreage and effort required. The hamlets consisted of a few blocks of gray, stone houses; the bleakness of the region was enlivened only by the red geraniums on the window ledges. The cheerless ground cautioned all living things to flee.

Inside of Drancy, twenty-two numbered doors led to one of the several dormitories located on each of the three floors. An overhead view showed a vast, enclosed square around which were four wings that housed the dormitories. The block of dormitories numbered from ten upward served as sleeping quarters for the inmates. The dormitories numbered one to ten housed those who were about to be deported.

At Drancy money bought everything except liberty. If you survived Drancy, it was said, you would succeed in business. Business was the business of living. Frantic bargaining continued day and night. For a price, one feigned illness and transferred to a hospital. For a price, one assumed the identity of someone scheduled for deportation who had suicided, and remained among the living prisoners for an indefinite period. Shrewd bargaining permitted even transfer to a camp in the unoccupied zone. The captors encouraged business arrangements that led, in the belief that families would be reunited, to transfer to camps more than a thousand miles away. When the dormitories were unfilled at sunrise or at sunset, trucks sped to Paris and a new roundup commenced. New arrivals came every day. The right price bought an extra ration of cabbage and beets, but no one seemed able to maintain the plumbing. Every few days a pipe broke, cutting off the water supply for the six, seven, eight thousand inmates. When there were plumbers in the barracks, no tools or lengths of pipe existed to make necessary repairs. When there was equipment, the plumbers had already been deported or transferred. Crude, makeshift repairs lasted only a few days.

Most of the infants at Drancy were assigned to dormitories numbered from one to ten. They were cared for by young girls and women assigned to these blocks. Every day nuns or nurses from the capital appeared with bottles of milk and small quantities of food for the infants. A metal drum was set up between two barracks and soiled diapers were boiled in it. When the water could not be changed because the plumbing had broken down, the same water was boiled over and over again. The liquid in the vessel became a thick, yellowish syrup. Occasionally one of the nuns or nurses poured a disinfectant into the tub.

In November, with the fields scraped clean of the last beet and cabbage leaf or when even the scrawny rats deserted the lifeless forest of the region, a large transport was arranged. Six hundred prisoners, including the oldest and youngest shivering in the chill behind the lowest-numbered doors, were assigned to a pleasant new community in the east. It was raining on the day they left and they ran to the trucks with their parcels and suitcases so as not to miss the transportation. Girls and women without children of their own carried aboard the tiny prisoners. The trucks drove to a railroad siding ten miles to the south. As the dreary train pulled away from the siding the trucks sped toward the capital for a new roundup.

It was dark when the steaming train slowed to a stop in Belfort. Most of the prisoners slept, huddled together to create warmth in the unheated cars. Those who were awake saw, by the dim light of the station, glistening piles of snow that grew higher. A group of girl scouts dressed in their dull-brown uniforms stood shivering on the station platform. They ran from car to car and tossed in bottles of drinking water, packages of cheese and bread. They had prepared bottles of heated milk and they handed them through the open windows to girls of their own age who held the infants in their arms.

"I used to be a scout!" one of the prisoners shouted.

"Courage!" came the reply of many. "Keep up your hope."

The train took more than an hour to load coal for the remainder of the trip. North of Belfort, the tracks turned, crawled alongside the mountains that merged in the valley where France, Switzerland, and Germany divided along imagined lines. The mountains then sloped into the Rhine Valley and became rugged hills.

There was no time for conversation between the girls in their brown uniforms and the prisoners. For older people who coughed and whimpered, they handed through the windows cold boiled potatoes, but there were metal cups of steaming broth.

"Out!" the guards of the train shouted. Whistles blew. A kerosene lantern swung in an arc, casting a pale-red light on the mounds of snow. Steam hissed from the undercarriage; a short blast sounded from the engine. The train heaved out of Belfort and headed laboriously into the snowcapped mountains.

Puffing slowly, rhythmically, the train wound around the narrow curve. A screech of the wheels and the train lurched as if biting into the mountainside and stopped. The jolt awakened all prisoners. Babies wailed. Dozens of flashlights and red-eyed lanterns darted about on the snowy slopes. The soldiers ran clumsily in the deep snow and shouted, swore, and shook snow from the barrels of their rifles as they accidentally tripped and fell. At the forward end, a section of rail was twisted upward, a serpentine sculpture glistening from the lights turned on it. Some of the heavy wooden ties were dislodged and splintered. Snowflakes curled around flashlight beams turned upward like moths clinging to icicles strung from the dark sky. It was bitterly cold. The French engine operator stood at the throttle, awaiting orders. A cigarette dangled from his lips.

A sharp crack whined from over the snow-covered

slopes. It echoed, and the sound amplified. A soldier dou-
bled over and flung his arms sideways. Flashlights turned
on him: a jagged hole bubbled dark blood from beneath
an eye. The lantern he had been holding spilled its contents and for a moment an orange flame licked across the
crest of a snow mound. The hole beneath the eye was
quickly filled by snow.

"Turn out your lights, you jackasses," a voice commanded. "Get all the prisoners out. Get them into columns
between the rails behind the last car. We shall go back to
the town. Prisoners will hold the flashlights and lanterns;
you march on the lower side. There will be no more
shooting after that."

"Out!" the soldiers shouted. They helped the prisoners
lower themselves from the cars so that they would not be
pushed back in the darkness over the side of the embankment and down the steep slopes. Some prisoners leaped
over the heads of their captors and tumbled, slid, and
rolled downward in the darkness. No light turned on. They
were ignored; presumably they would be buried under the
snow. Others who tripped and fell headlong downhill were
also ignored. A light invited further shooting. As if prear-
ranged, the bundled babies were handed carefully through
the windows and tossed in the darkness to a vague shadow
on the slope.

The march back to Belfort began. No count was taken
of either prisoners or soldiers. Perhaps a hundred prisoners had fled the train before the march. Most climbed
uphill in the direction from which the bullet came. There
they received food and shelter from a band of young
Frenchmen who would try to hide them. Some, with their
parcels and suitcases, chose a direction at random and ran
until the snow and the steepness of the slopes prevented
further movement and disappeared until the spring thaw.
Six of the young girls carried four of the tiny infants in
their arms and moved slowly down the treacherously steep
slope away from the abandoned train.

At a cleft in the mountainside, where wind had blown
away most of the snow, they found an outcropping of
stone, a ledge that would provide shelter. They huddled
about one another, keeping the infants inside their arms.

They smiled as they munched pieces of cheese and bread they had saved from the merciful gifts of the scouts.

A light flashed into the rock shelter. Gasps as hands covered mouths that wanted to scream. A voice: "Don't be afraid." A bright flashlight shone into the small space. The speaker was a boy of about nineteen. His cheeks were red, his eyes sparkled happily at them. "My name is Fernand. I'm Swiss. I was with the ones who blew up the rails. I want to take you to safety. To Switzerland." From a large rucksack strapped tightly to his back, he removed a few soft, warm blankets and some tins of meat, concentrated milk, some tablets of chocolate. They ate hurriedly, in silence. The babies slept.

Warmed and rested, they saw him gesture to leave. Moving away from the cleft, they followed in single file along a winding depression in the slope that seemed in the darkness to move toward the great dark shapes of higher slopes in the distance. They followed each other as if by some uncanny instinct, for there was no sound from the snow. The flashlight was kept off. Occasionally their guide told them in a soft voice that they should pause, lean against a firm embankment, and rest a few minutes, stretch their arms, and allow others to carry the infants. At last he said: "It will soon be sunrise. Ski patrols will be out. Just a little further there is a chalet. It is a priest's. He lives there in winter so he can ski from village to village. A storage room is carved into the mountain. I think we will be safe until it is dark again."

With the girls and infants safely inside the storage room, he looked about. Long shadows. Streaks of red in the openings between the mountains. The snow fell even more heavily than during the night. Their tracks were already obscured. Chances are, he thought, that most of the patrol would go to the vicinity of the marching column headed toward Belfort.

Except for taking turns caring for the infants, feeding them, cooing at them and talking quietly in fearful, subdued tones, the six girls spent the day sleeping or sharing and eating whatever food remained in the rucksack. They were younger than their youthful rescuer. The oldest of them was barely fourteen. It was awkward to engage him in conversation but their eyes begged him to speak, and for those who listened or who could understand, he said: "My father is a pastor in Porrentruy, near the frontier. He follows the line of the federal counselor: keep our borders closed, keep out the aliens, keep out the criminal elements. He's a kind man. A good man. But he's naive and narrow-minded about the realities of Europe. But there are others who oppose this view with all their heart. It is in the papers every day."

They had heard talk like this in their homes, heard their parents talk this way, and they recalled the newspapers on the living-room tables amidst the crumbs of the Saturday night sweets. They talked in the dark so that the batteries of the boy's flashlight would not be used up. They told him about the schools they attended before the summer vacation, about their friends, and that there had been talk about going to other countries. From time to time they removed their shoes and rubbed their feet to relieve the numbness.

At five o'clock in the morning they started out again. It was dark, windless; the heavy snow fell straight down. Around the chalet the snow hardened underfoot and the crunching of their steps caused their hearts to beat rapidly in fear of an unseen enemy. The black stillness made them feel safe and the hope of reaching Switzerland warmed them.

The first streaks of light showed the snow-peaked roofs of a row of houses. Smoke rose from the chimneys. The red and white Swiss flag hung limply from a pole in front of the nearest building.

"Is that Switzerland?" one of the girls asked breathlessly.

Fernand smiled. "Yes," he said. "But those are border police." He pointed to gray shapes that stood in front of the buildings. "Let's go up this slope. It's steep but not too bad if we help each other. There's a path on the other side where they won't see us."

"Halt!" a deep voice commanded.

A Swiss border guard appeared suddenly from behind them. "Illegal immigrants? Where are your papers?"

Fernand showed his papers and tried to explain. Three

days ago it was different. The policies for admitting the "illegals" varied from day to day and from one crossing point to another. Three days before they would have crossed at this point easily.

"We know who you are! You don't have to bother to explain anything. You," he said placing handcuffs around Fernand's wrists, "are under arrest. You are all under arrest."

Two more border guards puffed up the slope, grasped the boy under the shoulders, and led him off to one of the houses. Fernand's eyes sought the girls, sought to explain, begged for understanding and forgiveness. They stood before the border guard, impassive, their faces drained from exhaustion and cold. The four girls who carried the babies entreated the guard with trembling lips and tears.

"Child prostitutes!" he swore. "Degenerates. Where are your papers?"

Motionless, they said nothing.

"No papers? Back you go where you came from. Degenerate whores."

Several border policemen stood on the cleared road at the base of the slope, their rifles poised menacingly. To the right a road wound slowly down the mountain. In the distance hamlets, their chimneys breathing thin garlands of blue-tinged smoke. To the left a road into the mountains, the blankness of snow, the direction uncertain. They were marched to the red-and-white-striped poles that denoted the line that separated the countries. A hundred yards of slush-covered path separated them from another barrier on the other side, another cluster of houses, another pole with a sagging flag, from border troops in white uniforms.

"We're sorry," said one of the border guards. "Sorry, very sorry. We have young people like you in our homes. Babies too. But there have been too many. The order is very strict. Illegals must go back."

The instinct of flight. Does the blood carry a message of flight? Their eyes darted to the solemn faces of the guards, to the vague outline of the snow-topped forests ahead, to the narrow strip of land between the two frontiers. One last glance behind. The childlike geometry of rooftops carved in snow. Flight. Their knees quivered from the strain of the climb through the mountains, from hunger, from fear, from resignation. Halfway across the narrow stretch of land, the Swiss border guards left them and returned to the side of the red-and-white-striped poles. The girls walked the rest of the way unaccompanied. All this had happened before full daylight. As if the sun had dried up the sky, the snow stopped. Looking at the snow hurt the eyes. A black-and-red flag. Barking. The white-clad soldiers made gestures with their fingers as if calling animals.

The sudden and intense sunlight made the eyes of the infants blink wildly and tighten like fists. Wailing began for food.

"So!" a soldier exclaimed. "The little passengers return to continue their voyage. A little sightseeing on the side." There was raucous laughter from his companions.

"Go!" they spat, jerking rifle butts into the girls' shoulders. "Go! This path will take you to where you really want to go. Fast."

Weary, hungry, fearful, they dragged their feet in the slush, stooped, heads down. From a distance they could have been mistaken for a band of ragged, aged gypsies. Several hundred yards farther, where the road curved sharply, a cement blockhouse rose from a slope like an igloo. From a black slot in its smooth face a machine-gun barrel protruded. A cascade of orange flame, a shower of red sparks, a smell of something charred or burning. Some of them seemed to be lifted into the air before they fell. An infant screamed, then another and another as if an alarm had gone off. The girls writhed, groaning, their mouths vomiting slush and blood.

The sound of chains. The barking drew closer. The soldiers looked on, curious and amused. A pack of savage dogs leaped upon the writhing shapes, ripping through tattered clothes, tearing at white flesh. Sharp teeth sank into throats. Blood splayed onto the road in a pattern of red lace. Except for the growling and barking there was no sound. Their eyes glazed with frenzy, their jowls dripping shreds of human flesh, the pack withdrew to take docile positions by the heels of the white-clad soldiers. Chains were reattached to heavy leather collars. A soldier gathered up the chains and led the dogs to one of the houses. The remaining soldiers waited and lighted cigarettes. A small truck appeared. A snowplow blade was lowered, the remains pushed over the steep embankment, and soon indistinguishable from other mounds of snow. The blade raised, glistening in the bright sun.

A soldier grunted.

"There's one we didn't get."

"Where?"

"That. In the blanket."

One of them picked it up and pulled the corner of the blanket. A thin white face; eyes clenched like fists to keep out the sun.

"Phew!" the soldier holding the infant pinched his nose.

"Funny, the dogs wouldn't touch it."

"Probably stinks too bad."

"They can't keep their own clean!"

"What'll we do?"

"Throw it down with the others."

"No. That's not for me. You do it."

"That's not my stuff either."

"What is it? If it's male, we're okay. The order is to send all males back to the station."

The wrappings were peeled off. A warm stench of urine and dried stools. The little body was white, undernourished, the skin shriveled and festering where the waste had eaten into the belly and buttocks. Between the legs, a swollen, bluish scrotum, a penis.

"Male!"

"Not a Jew. See, nothing's been cut off."

"Good. Send him back." The child was wrapped and brought to one of the houses and placed on a chair. For a few minutes a heated argument ensued, followed by agreement to send the bundle back with the next batch of fleeing male fugitives. Back to the railroad station at Belfort.

Those who had been marched back to the station from the point in the mountains where the rails had been destroyed were gone. Within the day, the trains ran again, troops spread through the mountains to prevent a reoccurrence of such an incident.

There were others who sought a haven, all males, all

expulsed from border points in Switzerland by order of the federal government. From the Swiss press and pulpit cries arose to honor the moral laws of sanctuary, but to no avail. Illegals were sent back through narrow strips of land between the frontiers. Only a few hours' wait before a new train loaded.

The infant whom the dogs would not touch was handed to an illegal as he boarded a car and the train moved north toward the Rhine valley. There were many stopping-off places—infirmaries, hospitals, orphanages. By April 1942, when the spring rains poured down in torrents and swept away the first plantings and the farmers warned that food would be scarce, the infirmaries, hospitals, and orphanages yielded up the infant males that had been left in their care and delivered them to transportation centers at railway stations. In May, three thousand new passengers arrived at Auschwitz, most less than four years old. Every other one was thrown into a hand-drawn cart, pulled along a path that went to the right, and never seen again. Every other one was thrown into a hand-drawn cart that followed a path that went to the left, to the barracks. The children were handed over to women prisoners who had shaven heads, rags for clothes, women who wore ill-assorted men's shoes, women who wore a Red Cross patch stitched to the back of their blouses. This was the barracks area designated as the kindergarten and children's center; children arrived here from the transports or torn from their mothers' arms after birth in the camp.

There were rumors that the children from these barracks would show, as they grew, unmistakable signs of superior physique and high intelligence; eventually they would be adopted by loving parents from the homeland of the captors. In the barracks they received good nourishment and clean clothes. Every day, serious men and women with horn-rimmed glasses, high foreheads and a manner of speech that set them apart from soldiers and their superior officers, arrived in the barracks and told the women with shaven heads how to hold the children, how to feed them, how to speak to them, how to read to them, how to play with them.

The women with the shaven heads were teachers convicted of teaching false doctrine. In the kindergarten and children's center they taught as ordered, fed the children as ordered. And when the serious-looking men and women who were professors of pedagogy left the barracks, the teachers held the children to their bosoms, kissed them, fondled their heads and arms and whispered nonsense words, all contrary to orders.

One of them held the littlest child of all, frail, still undernourished in spite of adequate food, silent except when in pain. This was the illegal male that was rejected by the dogs.

"What shall we call him?" asked one of the women of the kindergarten.

"Abelard," her companion answered, laughing.

"Why that?"

"It's a name from a love story."

"They would have a fit if we called him that. No. Another."

"The rules say the name should begin with the letter of the month. M. It's got to be M."

"Manfred."

"Fine."

She wrote the name on a card and recorded the child's measurements and birthmarks.

The child's diaper was changed, the fresh one taken from a high pile of them in many colors. They had been cut from cotton garments that once were shirts and dresses.

Chapter 4

LEON AND ROSE

The blackness of her hair, the darkness of her skin made her eyes larger and more luminous than they actually were. Her wide, full lips changed color, from deep pink to purple. Cyanosis. She looked without seeing, smiled without smiling. It was a child's look of indifferent acceptance.

"She's not afraid," Leon said, trying to console his wife.

"She's smiling," Rose said. The movements of her eyes, her lips, tried to elicit a sign of recognition from the child. The cellophane sheets of the oxygen tent barely moved.

"She doesn't know, does she, Doctor?"

The doctor shook his head. A hubbub erupted in the corridor. He moved the three-paneled screen that served as a door and stuck his head out and looked for someone he could tell to be quiet. He saw animated movement and heard loud, almost shouted fragments of conversation. The rising voices violated the many placards that called for silence. No one noticed the finger placed against his lips. He stepped into the corridor and caught a nurse by the arm.

"I have a very sick patient. What's all the noise for?"

"I'm sorry, Doctor. Germany has just invaded Poland. War. There's going to be a world war." She freed herself from his grasp and ran toward the nurses' station.

Neither Leon or Rose was aware of the commotion.

Each stood on a side of the oxygen tent and waited for the last signs of life to fade from the twelve-year-old under the transparent sheet.

"My baby," Rose sighed, her cheeks trembling.

The doctor returned to the bedside, angry that he could not end the commotion.

"Can you give her one more day of life?" Leon asked. "Just one?"

The doctor placed an arm on Leon's shoulder. "We've done everything. Everything. It's not in our power any more. We can only wait for the end."

Noise could be heard again from the corridor. Slowly the child's eyes closed. As if struck by a pin, the legs jerked, then were still. The lips parted as if sucking in one last gulp of air, then closed. Repose and contentment after a kiss, then serenity. Complete serenity.

The doctor shut the valve of the green oxygen tank that stood to the rear of the bed. He carefully removed the cellophane folds. He placed the chrome end of his stethoscope on the child's chest where breasts had not yet formed. He raised, then lowered an eyelid.

"She's gone to sleep," he said softly. "There was no pain. It was all peaceful."

Rose's body stiffened as she withheld the wild sobs that shrieked inside. "My baby. My baby." She leaned over and kissed the child's eyes. Her husband stroked the long black tresses for one last time.

The doctor pressed a button on the end of a cord that hung at the side of the bed next to the medical charts. It was a signal to nurses and orderlies: they knew what to do and reacted immediately. But they didn't. Simple customary things were not happening as expected. He strode to the nurses' station prepared to make a scene. But too many were about and the group included not only nurses and orderlies but internes and residents as well. A scene would be badly taken. He overheard snatches of conversation.

"If I had a German patient, I know what I'd do."

"Same for me."

"Nurse," he whispered to the supervisor.

"Have you heard?" she asked.

"Yes," he replied. "My patient, the Howard child, she just expired. Would you—?"

"I'm sorry, Doctor. I'll take care of things right away." She moved away from the gathering.

White-smocked orderlies prepared to remove the bed from the oxygen room. The man and woman held hands and watched.

"Leon, promise me something."

"Anything, Rose. Anything."

"Promise me we will adopt another child. No matter what."

"I promise. No matter what."

The homes in the neighborhood of Beth David Hospital were mainly one- and two-story brick houses. Rows of hedges grew thick and green. Late-summer flowers bloomed from the small patches of garden in front of each house. Pink roses and yellow roses seemed everywhere. Their fragrance hung over the streets. Families loaded packages on car roofs and prepared to desert Brooklyn for the long-awaited Labor Day weekend. Leon and Rose had already canceled their reservations. On this quiet, late summer morning, they walked hand in hand toward their home without speaking. If she had lived another week, there could have been a final, joyous holiday weekend.

Since the summer of 1929 when they had adopted Ada Lynn, they had spent every Labor Day weekend at Mountainview, a small hotel in the Catskills. The proprietor, a distant cousin of Rose's, singled them out for special hospitality and provided special treats for Ada Lynn. By the time she was three, a shetland pony was kept in its own colorful, miniature stable, reserved for the child. It was referred to as Ada Lynn's pony. When a calf was born at the hotel farm, it was named Ada Lynn's calf. The child fetched fresh eggs from the henhouse and ran with them to the hotel kitchen. She annoyed the maids by playing hide-and-seek in the linen closets and was never chastised when she sat on the musicians' laps during evening performances and made faces at the guests.

Abraham Breen, proprietor of Mountainview, was

grateful to his remote cousins in ways that knew no bounds. Leon had loaned him money regularly, from the first crushing blow of the stock-market collapse in the autumn of 1929 throughout the difficult Depression years until the first signs of recovery in 1938. Not only did Leon lend money to keep Mountainview from bankruptcy but he loaned generously to Abraham Breen to buy up small hotels and small farms that adjoined his property, places forced into bankruptcy. They could, should, and must be bought, Leon said, and the properties cost next to nothing. By Labor Day 1939, Mountainview totaled more than a thousand acres and, thanks to Leon, enough money was available to pay an abundant supply of cheap labor to build additional wings to the hotel, tennis courts, riding stables, and maintain vast, trim gardens and lawns. "The worst is over," Leon told him. "With less competition and recovery you'll have a unique resort city instead of just another hotel."

They reached their house. It resembled the other twenty on the street: the same five white limestone steps leading up a stoop to the front door, the same green hedges, the same blue-and-white hydrangeas. Boys in knickers roller-skated noisily on the street; they cursed and shouted; young girls jumped rope and sang jingles. Except for the lead numbers cemented to the brick wall beside the front door, the houses were identical. Leon had been born there and lived there after his father and mother died. Rose was born in an identical house farther up the street. When they married, she moved into Leon's house. With the money Leon made manufacturing mirror reflectors for car headlights, they could have moved into a large house in the uncrowded suburbs, or into a large apartment on Riverside Drive, even Central Park West or Fifth Avenue. But they preferred to raise Ada Lynn on the quiet streets where they grew up, send her to the same public school where they were classmates, have her taught by the same teachers. They knocked against the child's bicycle as they entered the vestibule.

Louis Lieberg was already there and had let the doctor in. On the round dining-room table two bottles of champagne stood beside a bowl of artificial fruit.

"So you've met," Leon said.

The two men nodded.

"This is a medical prescription," said Dr. Mowiss as he opened one of the bottles. "To ease the pain. To make the heart lighter again. I brought some cakes, too." He poured and handed each the bubbling, amber-filled glasses.

He lifted his glass and offered a toast: "May we all live long, healthy lives."

They drank. Only Rose's hands were unsteady; a spray of liquid fell from her glass to the carpet.

"Drink heartily," Dr. Mowiss told Rose. "It's good for everything. When a patient of mine has only a short time left, I break open a bottle of champagne or a good bottle of cognac and we drink. It's a good feeling. You go to sleep with a light heart and with a sense of joy."

"That's how I want to go," Rose said, emptying the glass with a gulp. Later, when she was alone, she cried, tore her clothes, cursed her barrenness.

Her glass was filled again.

"Dr. Mowiss," she said. "If you happen to be by my side when I go, I want champagne just like this."

Her voice sounded giddy. After almost three days of not eating, the champagne produced euphoria.

"For me, cherry brandy," said Leon. "You?" he asked, looking at his childhood friend and attorney Louis Lieberg. "What's your preference?"

Lieberg smacked his lips and refilled his glass. "Champagne, I guess. Like this."

"It's going to be a long while before we get imported champagne again," Dr. Mowiss mused. He undid the foil and wire on the second bottle.

"If we had known," Rose said with difficulty.

"What?" Leon asked, his eyes apprehensive. She had been tense, reserved. Held it all back. It wouldn't last.

"If we had known sooner that she had a rheumatic heart. Something could have been done. She would be alive instead of. . . ."

"Come on Rose," he pleaded.

"No. Don't ignore me. Answer me." Her voice became shrill, on the verge of hysteria.

"How could we tell?" Leon asked. "We adopted her so fast." His eyes sought help from Lieberg and the doctor.

"Sometimes," Lieberg began helplessly; he stopped talking.

"Even if she were born of your flesh, Mrs. Howard," Dr. Mowiss's manner and voice soothed and comforted, "it would not have been possible to know everything. Children can't always express what bothers them until it's too late. When symptoms do pop up so that they're visible, the situation may be beyond help. Children, how can they express subtle things? But doctors make mistakes, big ones. Sometimes we look at a badly bruised knee and think it's from a fall when it may really be a rare sign of an enlarged heart. How can we tell? It's damned difficult, especially in children."

"It's God's will," Leon said.

"I prefer to think that it's the work of the devil," the doctor replied, "the devil of our own ignorance. The devil of our vanity. We want so much to be in command of our life and our fate that we destroy ourselves by tampering with nature, by not allowing things to happen as they will. We do more damage in medicine by doing than by leaving things alone, but that happens out of ignorance, the ignorance of not knowing when to leave matters alone. God is no meddler."

"It's quite different in the law," Louis Lieberg said, fingering his gray pin-striped suit. Like his boss, Brooklyn's gang-busting district attorney, Lieberg was short, trim, and dapper. "Everything is precise and spelled out. In law we have to meddle because people don't obey laws or live up to contracts according to nature's will."

The talk distracted Rose. She sipped more champagne. Lieberg's figure blurred. Was this the man who, with Leon's money, wanted to become a judge as a stepping stone to higher office? A blur, a confused web of lines talked words she couldn't understand.

"We've got to meddle or law dissolves and anarchy steps in. That's what's happening right now. Look at this neighborhood. A good neighborhood, but because we've been easy on hoodlums the neighborhood goes down. Now we can still leave the house without locking the doors, on

55

hot nights we can sleep in front of the house, but in twenty years it'll be a jungle. It's got to become a jungle eventually because people are losing respect for law and not enough of us are meddling where it counts. The war is going to speed it up."

"What war?" Rose asked, bleary-eyed.

Dr. Mowiss poured more champagne.

"You haven't heard?"

"Haven't heard what?"

"Germany invaded Poland today. It was on the radio. Soon there will be a world war."

"America, also?"

"Not right away," Lieberg replied. "But we can't stay neutral for too long. I think that we should go in right away. You know what Hitler's been doing in Germany. People laugh and say we Jews always exaggerate, but the facts will come out." He looked at the doctor uncertainly. He wondered whether Mowiss was a Jew. Many non-Jewish doctors, he thought, were affiliated with Beth David Hospital.

Rose's voice was hoarse: "The League of Nations should stop it. Right now."

The three men smiled at her unworldliness.

She was calm, Leon thought. Calmer than she had been in the past three days since the crisis began. She wouldn't break down, yet. He said: "Louis, you will take care of the funeral arrangements?"

"Of course." A wave of the hand. A gesture indicated that it was beyond question that their oldest friend and attorney accepted the painful duties.

"Rose and I want to establish a living memorial for Ada Lynn. It's going to be a ten-year pledge to the hospital to build a children's wing. Even if one life is saved. . . ."

"Very generous!" Lieberg exclaimed.

Dr. Mowiss smiled.

"Wonderful of you, Leon. But you don't have that kind of money."

"I know," Leon said. "Not at the moment. That's why I want to do it over ten years. For me, it's the purpose of living and working. I've been offered a nice price for my plant. A terrific figure. If I take it all in one shot the tax people will eat it up. If I spread it over ten years, half will go to meet the pledge for a children's wing, and with the other half I've got some ideas for going into real estate. The business will grow terrifically, especially because of what's happening in Europe. Every year a bigger percentage of the profits'll come to me—for the hospital and for the real-estate thing. Business worries I don't want any more; I'm getting too old to carry them. And what do we need the aggravation for? How does it sound, now, Louis?"

"Sounds all right."

"You'll take care of the papers?"

"Of course." The same assured, taken-for-granted tone.

"And you, Doctor," he said and made no effort to recall his name, "you have been a great comfort to us the past few terrible days. We feel good knowing that you gave her everything possible. We would like you to be head of the children's wing."

"I'm flattered," he replied, holding up the champagne bottle to the light. It was empty. "You have the wrong man. But I really appreciate the generous gesture. I can't. First, I'm not the administrative type. Second, a man to head up a pediatric wing should be a specialist and a much younger man. We're all about forty-five, forty-six. Too old to start big responsibilities. I'm not an old fart, but going into pediatrics is not my dish. General practice was bad enough and I wish to hell I could find my way out of it. Pretty soon I may even want to get married."

"There's something else." Leon's eyes fixed on Lieberg.

"I'm afraid of what you're going to ask, Leon," said the dapper attorney.

"Speak, already," Rose cried, her cheeks trembling.

"We want," he stammered, "to adopt another child."

"Leon, Rose," said the lawyer, "you are my dearest friends. There's nothing in the world I wouldn't gladly do for you. But an adoption! It was damn near impossible ten years ago. Now you're ten years older. Forty-six, both of you. No agency will do it."

Leon turned to his wife with a look that begged for understanding and a release from the hasty promise. Her eyes turned to Dr. Mowiss; they burned. The question was sharply clear.

"I agree. I won't say impossible, but it's close to it. It's not a matter of love or money. They're just plain rigid."

She jumped from the sofa. An accusing finger darted toward each of them.

"So, you, Doctor, are allowed to make mistakes with life. And you, Louis, are going to be a famous, important, and powerful politician. And you, my Leon, you're going to do God's work and be a philanthropist and dedicate a hospital, then invest in real estate. What about me? Me? A woman of forty-six. I'm nothing? I'm washed up with life and living? I don't count for anything? The future is only for men? What about me? Ten years ago we were too old to adopt a child. Now we're even older. I can't accept it. We must have a child. Somewhere someone must know how it should be done. I don't accept that the future says to me 'no children.' No, I don't accept it. You're lying because you're lazy and don't care. My god, my god! There are no tears left inside of me."

"We can give our love to many children in other ways, Rose, darling."

She shook her head violently. The storm drew nearer, about to be unleashed.

Leon turned to Dr. Mowiss. "Will you help us?"

"Someday, yes. I give you my word." He held out his hand and Leon grasped it firmly between his own.

"Louis? You?" Leon asked his lifelong friend.

"Be realistic, Leon. We have to accept the way life is."

"No!" Rose screamed. "Life is not the way it is, it's the way we want it. Don't betray me."

Leon placed his arms around her trembling body. Each part tensed and shook with brief spasms.

"I think we should go and not talk any more today."

"No!" she screamed.

"What can I say?" said Louis Lieberg with a helpless shrug. "Someday. Yes, someday."

Pained and embarrassed, they left quickly.

"You see, Rose darling," Leon said comfortingly as he

eased back into the couch. "Someday. Someday, we'll have another child."

Then her soul burst and she cried uncontrollably.

They walked in the cool shadows of the elevated train, silently, as if trying to decipher the meaning of the grating clatter of the steel wheels against the rails.

"You going back to the hospital?"

Mowiss nodded. "For one last time."

"This army thing you mentioned—aren't you too old to get mixed up? There's enough to do right here in the city."

"A few years ago I was asked by some of my patients to join them and go as a doctor to Spain. They were young, wonderful boys. Great spirits, their heads filled with beautiful ideals. I didn't go. I regret it very much. Their bodies were brought back, some of them, only a few months ago. Had I been there, I don't know what I would have done for international politics, but I could have perhaps saved a few lives. I didn't realize that Spain was the beginning of a new dark age. Even though it was only months ago, only last year, it was another age. We're living now, in the kingdom of now, and we have to see that this kingdom survives because in this kingdom we are all royalty, all kings and queens. Royalty has obligations. I've decided that this new war may be the one to end war for all time or end life for all time. I'm going to take a few months to wind up my practice and enlist. If I return alive, I want to do something else besides medicine. I'm not sure."

Lieberg looked at him disbelievingly. They were in fact, he thought, too old for the adventures of youth. At forty-six they had reached the age of command and responsible authority, not fighting or following. A few years as judge, then a safe election to sweep him in as district attorney, afterward, state attorney general. It had been carefully laid out. Preserve and carry out the law and there is no war, no chaos, no anarchy. A disgruntled bachelor doctor who craved for the adventures of youngsters!

"You're not serious." The champagne had warped his lips into a sardonic smile.

Angrily Dr. Mowiss snapped: "Damned serious."

Even when the intense August sunlight glanced through the ties, the pupils of Mowiss's eyes remained large and black.

"Look," he snapped, "there's enough to knock in the law from now to doomsday. That's your problem. Medicine's mine. And it's been a horrible disappointment. Eight out of ten people don't need a doctor; one out of ten can't be helped at all and the other one is lucky if you get to him at the right time. The battlefield has got to be the right time. It's only when there's a real choice of life or death that medicine matters. I want to be there to make the choice."

"You don't believe that everyone has a right to live, a right that doesn't depend on your choice?"

Mowiss laughed. "Nature's a freak show and no one likes freaks. If we didn't flush them down the toilet there'd be a human monster on every street corner. If only we could, each one of us, grab onto a life at the right time, at the lucky time and fill it with understanding and the right kind of love, there'd be no damn dictators or war."

"You seem confident that you know what that right kind of love is. For me, certainty is something negotiable."

"No. I don't. But I'm going to find out."

Chapter 5

JOURNEYS

One day, the world seemed about to end.

Suddenly, the purple plum-colored smoke that belched from the four smokestacks of the crematoria disappeared. Suddenly a glow no longer tinged the night sky red. The stench of putrefaction that clung to everything for miles around vanished—suddenly. One day, there was no roll call, neither in the morning when the sun broke through the haze nor in the evening when the damp chill began. Prisoners who collapsed lay where they fell; work gangs tossed them into carts and removed them to the pyramid of still-breathing corpses. Suddenly whips and truncheons no longer were visible. One day, as the world seemed about to end, a new kind of activity commenced and the authorities carried out the new work differently. No one screamed commands or crushed the skulls of those who did not—or could not—obey; they directed the new tasks and took part, themselves, in the work.

"Spread it. Spread it!" they shouted and wielded shovels themselves. Instead of rifles, they carried rakes. Those who could work accompanied the guards to the broad fields beyond the camp and spread gray ashes delivered by carts from the camp.

One day, the familiar faces of the guards were less. Many vanished—suddenly. And suddenly, the high, brick chimneys crumbled to the ground as sledge hammers clanged against steel plates. Chunks of jagged red brick and mortar were lifted into trucks that drove past the high wrought-iron gates.

The world did not end that day, but the next day, with again no roll call, seemed from another age. A continuous stream of trucks filled with prisoners and only a few guards in each left the camp during the day and at night, returning with only a driver; then they were loaded again and immediately departed.

By the end of the upside-down day and through the following day, two things, for all who had the strength to speak, were spoken of: no food remained in the camp and the front edged closer.

The iron sheds to the rear of the administrative compound that housed provisions for the guards were open, but no sacks of any kind were visible. In their feverish activity to move things and people, the uniformed guards grunted: it's coming closer; on both sides it's coming closer.

During the day and night farmers continuously came to the gates and offered exchanges: potatoes for clothing. The clothing warehouse was forty feet wide, one hundred feet long, and fifteen feet high. Bundles of clothing were crammed from cement floor to iron rafters. No matter how much exchanged for food, the pile seemed untouched, its density undiminished. From behind the high concrete wall that separated the administration compound from the camp yards, from behind the wall where only days before the sound of machine guns and screams sounded the day long, rose long curls of smoke and pointed tongues of orange flame; documents, records, letters, memorandums were reduced to ashes. All who could still hear, could still speak, heralded the approach of the front. Many who lived could not move; they waited for the end. Had they known of the revolutionary changes that occurred, they would have remained indifferent and immobile.

On the second day, the electric current that flowed through the triple rows of mesh fences stopped. The frothing, whining German shepherds that ran the length of the outer alley between the second and third fence were chained and dragged off howling and snarling. On the night of the second day holes appeared in the fences and some said inmates had escaped. But none were surprised, none concerned. How many? No matter. Gone! Where? No matter. The screeching alarm that had sounded frequently in past days remained silent. Troops did not race through the gates to capture runaways. With the end of the roll calls, all counting ceased. The signs above the showers were removed and smashed with axes, then burned under the cauldrons to heat the stagnant, filthy water used to cook soup. The signs on the railroad siding that ran adjacent to the north arm of the camp—signs that greeted, signs that described a country station sounding like a resort town—were ripped down and burned on the spot. Prisoners who worked, who could still work, were gradually emptied from the camp and driven away in trucks. To factories, it was said. Some prisoners who worked walked through the gates of the camp, without tools, without guards; they walked casually as if on a country stroll, and nobody cared. Only the sick and the children stayed in or near the barracks.

On the fifth day, about twenty trucks drove through the camp and up close to the children's barracks; motors hummed.

Out and into the trucks, the soldiers commanded. Hurry!

Almost a hundred children to each truck. Motors growled. The spring mud on the road flew into the air. The convoy drove for several hours before it slowed and finally stopped. The roads were impassable. Thousands, tens of thousands, of soldiers jammed the roads; many lay on the banks of the road and looked tired, curious, or unhappy. They waited for orders to move and were indifferent to the trucks. After a while access to a smaller road was cleared and the trucks moved slowly, carefully, across the crowded intersection dense with puzzled soldiers.

Movement on the narrower road lasted for less than an hour, before the scene repeated itself. Trucks and equipment had bogged down; men waited for orders. A way was again cleared and a still smaller road was taken until the motors of the trucks spluttered and went dead. The metal containers strapped to the front of the trucks were empty. The soldiers in the cabs of the trucks, and those who had been riding in the rear with the children, jumped to the road. The tailgates lowered. The soldiers shouted in a hodgepodge of different languages:

"Go! Leave the trucks. You're free."

Children fell over each other; they scratched, slapped, pinched, shouted, bit. Once out of the trucks, hundreds ran across the muddy fields like rabbits that fled hunters. But they were not the hunted. No one came after them. They were free. In the ditches, by the trunks of trees, wounded soldiers who had wandered away from their regiments lay dead or in comas. Some of the children ransacked their clothing. A wristwatch that could be exchanged for bread, a cigarette for a whole sausage, a gun for real soup with pieces of chicken floating in it; small bony hands emptied blood-encrusted pockets. Some found many cigarettes, lighted them, and sat on the corpses and watched other children who fought with one another for possession of a bayonet, watched a soldier's life ebb from his bewildered eyes. Many discarded the rags worn about their feet and put on, instead, heavy soldier's shoes stuffed with articles that could be exchanged.

Many others, the smaller ones, slipped down, jumped, or fell from the tailgate and sat down beside the trucks and waited to be told what to do. Wide eyes searched the strange surroundings looking for wire fences, guards, women with shaven heads to ask them to do things, call them to bring their tin cups to the soup pots, tell them to go to sleep. They listened for whistles, sirens, gunshots that signaled times to do things; they listened for the moans of the dying, weeping for the dead, but they heard only the shouts of children running through the fields, arguments for the possession of an object taken from a dead soldier. Some in groups of three and four walked hand in hand along the road until they could no longer be seen. Others, after a while, merged with the forest into which they had walked. Go! the soldiers had shouted.

They went in all directions; by nightfall, few remained near the empty, useless trucks. The younger ones waited the longest and, after a while, chased after the footsteps of the older ones. Other clusters of children waited until one moved away, then they followed. Without words, without direction, without reason. Who first went forward? How is it possible to know? Did anyone know that the children who set out toward the forest would live yet another day? Or die? Did anyone know that crossing the field on the lower rather than the higher side would result in being picked up by a convoy of trucks and transported back to the very camp from which they had been taken and told to go? They went in the direction their feet pointed or followed someone or a group whose feet pointed in one rather than another direction.

One girl, black stubble growing from her recently shaven head, leaped from the truck the moment the order was given to go and stumbled behind some bushes on the side of the road. She crouched and waited. Soon she heard the scraping sounds of rocks and branches from the hillock above her: another child scrambled up the slope to join a group of fleeing children, fell and rolled down the slope and stopped by the thick bushes a few feet from where she hid. A girl. Blonde stubble on her head. Because she was tired, perhaps because her foot had been injured, she merely sat up and looked about and made no movement to reclimb the hill and rejoin the others.

They looked at each other angrily.

The one with black eyes and dark skin spoke first:

"Why don't you go with them?" She jabbed a finger toward the hill's crest.

"Because I don't want to. That's why."

"Go away."

"I will not."

"Go away. I'll beat you." She grasped a clump of prickly shrubs as if to make good her threat.

"Beat me. I'll stay here as long as I want."

"They'll find out at roll call that you're not supposed to be here."

"Stupid," the blonde replied. "There's not going to be any roll call. Not any more. We're outside. There's no more camp. We're outside."

Their speech was a mixture of several languages. The words were slang words learned from whoever slept in the bunk above or below, whoever brought food, whoever gave orders, and this often changed.

"Where are you from?"

"Barracks B fifteen, alley four."

"Before?"

"I don't know."

"Same with me."

"What's your name?"

"Helga. But in the barracks they made it Lussiya."

"Ugh. I don't like that."

"Call me another name."

"No. I won't call you anything."

"What's your name?"

"They called me Naomi. I like that name."

"Where should we go?"

"I don't know yet. Let's just stay."

"For how long?"

"You're stupid. We'll stay until we go. That's how long we'll stay."

When the soldiers' bodies were picked clean and the children gone from the vicinity of the trucks, only one small child stood on the side where an older child had placed him. He wore trousers cut down from the bundles of men's clothes in the warehouse. He looked as if he wore a dark skirt. His face turned in the direction of the shrubs behind which they waited. He sensed they were there, but did not approach. From the shirt without sleeves, more rag than shirt, long bony arms protruded—frail, sickly, and undernourished.

The girl with the blonde hair and blue eyes shouted: "Hey, little piece of whorehouse filth. You."

At the familiar words of the captors, he stopped trembling.

The plump child imitated her companion: "Hey, filthy parasite, do you hear?"

He leaned his body toward the shrubs; his legs remained rooted to the muddy road.

"Scum of the earth, come here!"

The command. He flattened the discolored palms of his hands against bony thighs and approached in small steps.

They parted the shrubs and entered the road. The spindly legs poked out of the oversize trousers.

"You stay with us, you piece of nothing," Naomi said.

"Maggot on a dungheap, you stay with us," her companion said gleefully.

The boy nodded and approached them like a cat seeking a master's leg to rub against.

"We are a work team," Naomi declared. "We work together, we eat together, we sleep together. Understood?"

"Understood," said the girl with the large dark eyes.

"Work team," the boy repeated.

It was not hard to satisfy their needs. Wherever they went, near farms, in the rubble of villages and towns, they found many dead people: soldiers, shopkeepers, factory workers, policemen, bicyclists, students, people who defied description. If the bodies had not been scavenged before they arrived, they always found something to eat: bread crusts, dried sausage, a tin of ground fish, cheese. There were plenty of items that could be exchanged with farmers and shopkeepers for food: watches, combs, cigarettes, guns, knives, wallets with photographs, shirts, shoes, knapsacks, rope, matches. There were always places to stay, sometimes, for days at a time, away from bombs and explosions and fires. There were abandoned cellars where they could always find pieces of candle to light. Sometimes a slab of a building would fall across a bomb crater and form a comfortable shelter; blankets and pillows were easily found and the three did not carry many things as they traveled. In a soldier's pocket they found a piece of perfumed soap and washed with it. Once they found a small bottle of perfume and doused themselves, laughing at the odor that followed them.

As the weather warmed they peeled a change of clothing from corpses. When many, many people foraged in the rubble of cities, almost no food was to be found and they walked into the forests where there were bodies that had not yet yielded their possessions. When there was nothing in the forests they made their way to the farms and these became increasingly difficult places to find food. Even watches and guns could not be exchanged for the smallest morsel of food; had they food themselves, the farmers would have bartered their own possessions for it. These were farms without animals, with sheds and cellars emptied of provisions; many others had been fed by whatever remained before the three of them arrived. There had been deserting soldiers, families who fled the cities, and bands of older children who beat the farmers and searched their houses for scraps.

When the three approached a farm even during the balmy days at the height of the planting season, often the farmers were not planting, for there was no seed; instead they were in the fields combing the furrows from the previous autumn, searching for edible roots, perhaps a potato not struck from the soil, perhaps under a pile of mulch a small cabbage that had not fully rotted through the winter. The farmers did not always chase them away with long wooden rakes or pitchforks; sometimes they merely showed the children their empty hands and invited them to go into the fields to find whatever they could for themselves. Even birds and the small rodents that usually inhabit farm areas had all but vanished.

They were in a city in which most of the people had either been killed or had fled. They were in the cellar of an abandoned hat shop. They slept most of the day on mattresses they had made from artificial flowers and milliner's lace. They spent the day in sleep since it was easier to search for food at night when they could be less easily seen. It was warm and sunny in the cellar, for a wide window opened on the street; in the daytime it was quiet since the front had already passed through the city. They went to sleep in the early morning when the sun rose and they were hungry and impatient for the night to come so that they could dig into some still-smoldering shop and find food that someone had overlooked or hidden.

On such a day three soldiers entered the cellar. When they touched the children's foreheads, smiles lit their faces. The children awakened with expressions of alarm. The soldiers towered above them. No place to run. They jumped from the mattresses and kicked, scratched the soldiers, shouted obscenities in many languages. The soldiers laughed and amiably held the children at arm's length to prevent themselves from being bitten.

"Friends," said one of the soldiers.

"Friends," chimed in the other two.

The three children backed into the corner. Artificial flowers were strewn all over the floor and had caught on the soldiers' uniforms.

One reached into a knapsack and withdrew half a loaf of dark bread and a stick of sausage.

The children's eyes gleamed.

"Here," he said, holding forth the offering.

The children grabbed at the food and threw themselves on what remained of the makeshift mattresses, devouring the soldier's offering.

By nightfall they slept on black military blankets in a school building that became administration center and dormitory for hundreds of children found in cellars, bomb craters, and forests.

September 1948

Chapter 6

THE REUNION

It took a year from the time Ida Kaminets visited, showing them photographs of children, until they were escorted into the office of the director of the children's camp at St. Fernan. Ida Kaminets had given them every assurance short of a guarantee that their age presented no obstacle. On the transatlantic crossing from New York they talked of little else. At fifty-five they could have had grandchildren; the twelve-year-old daughter they hoped they would adopt would be mistaken for their grandchild. "So people will make the mistake," Rose said consolingly to her husband. "Once, twice, they'll make the mistake, then no one will pay attention."

"But what kind of a life can we make for a child?" Leon asked, torn between fulfilling his promise and giving up the adoption idea because of their age.

"As good a life as any mother and father can give a child," she answered calmly.

At first they had expressed only mind interest in Ida Kaminets's proposition. They would have to review the matter with Judge Lieberg because of the legal questions involved. The first snapshots showed mainly boys, and the few girls in the pictures seemed young, much younger than the child they had in mind. A year later, they made their decision quickly when they received a package in the mail with many snapshots, among them the face of a child who

70

could have been Ada Lynn herself. It was on that day that they bought tickets, packed their bags, made preliminary arrangements with the principal of Hartley School so that the child would be enrolled in a class with children her own age, and had their housekeeper Cassie prepare a room for their daughter. They were certain it would all work out the way they wanted.

Leon was gruff, businesslike. It would have been better, he told his wife, to make all arrangements through lawyers, see the child in New York, and reserve the right to decline. By coming to France, they had left themselves little room for a change of heart. It all seemed too definite.

Rose's hand trembled as she handed the single snapshot to the camp director. He recognized the face, and pulled a folder from a file cabinet. "A pleasant child," he said. He scanned the sheets of paper. "We have given her the name Deborah. Like many of the children here, she came to us under irregular circumstances. There were no documents, you understand—hasty border crossings and all that. She claims to know nothing of her origin and is indifferent to any name. She accepted the name Deborah not unpleasantly, but indifferently. It will be desirable not to ask questions about the past. Many of these children have lived through an indescribable hell. She has been here about six months and was in a group that had been transferred from one camp to another in the American and French Zones. That's all we know. Medically, overweight as you will see. But a genuinely pleasant girl who is very helpful and well behaved. Shall I bring her in?"

Rose smiled. Leon tried to catch her eyes, hoping thereby to caution her not to rush into things, to wait.

They did not converse as they waited for the camp director to return with the child. Rose told herself to control her emotions. She would communicate to the child a feeling that she was wanted by both of them, would be loved as their real child, that America offered everything she ever dreamed of. Leon looked out the window at the trees and the green hills beyond.

The camp director entered his office, quietly closing the door. He was alone.

"Deborah is just outside. I wanted you to know that

should you change your mind about Deborah, there are
many, many wonderful children here. In particular, there's
a seven-year-old boy. We have given him the name
Michel. In America it would be Michael."

Rose tensed in her chair. She sat stiffly, hardly heard
the director's words, imagined she saw the waiting child
through the door.

"A boy!" Leon said. He stroked his chin. A novel idea.
For a moment he wondered why, in all the years since
Ada Lynn's death, they had never mentioned a boy to one
another.

"Bring her in," Rose said curtly.

The director showed the child into the office; his hand
rested gently on the girl's shoulder.

In a mixture of French and German, the director
presented Deborah to her prospective parents. He inter-
preted the conversation that followed in the same manner.

The child looked at them sullenly, unaware that the expressions on their faces were inspired by her uncanny resemblance to a child who died nine years before. Neither
Leon or Rose denied the remarkable resemblance. Their
eyes devoured the child and they spoke hurriedly to the
camp director, waiting impatiently for the interpretation
and the child's answers.

"We are from New York. In America. We have no children."

As the director translated, the child shrugged.

"We have a lovely home and would like to make a
home there for you."

The girl called Deborah shifted clumsily from one foot
to the other.

"We would like to love you and hope that in time you
will love us as a child of our own."

Deborah looked bewildered. When scores of children
left the camp each week in colorful busses unaccompanied
by men carrying weapons, much discussion ensued in the
barracks to the effect that the ones who left were going to
wonderful places with kind, loving people to help them.
But they had heard these words many times before and in
many languages. And each week scores of new arrivals
appeared. What were these people asking?

"We would like you to be our own daughter. We would like to be your own mother and father. We would like you to come with us, today, to America."

He repeated their words several times for the child kept repeating: *"Je ne comprends pas."* "No understand."

There was a brief, almost heated exchange between the child and the director. He turned to Leon and Rose with a look of troubled helplessness.

"She says that she will go with you on one condition."

"A condition?" Leon exclaimed. "A condition!"

"What kind of condition?" Rose asked simply, unable to take her eyes off the child's heavy dark-skinned face.

Leon flared: "What kind of condition? This is no business deal. We came to adopt a child and the child wants to make a condition. Did you ever hear of such a thing?"

"Leon, please don't raise your voice," Rose pleaded.

"It's unusual," the director said. "But remember that these children at St. Fernan have had to learn to drive hard bargains merely to stay alive."

"All right," Leon said grudgingly. "What's the condition?"

The child stood rooted in front of the director's desk. Rose's eyes were hypnotically directed at Deborah's—hoping to draw the child to her, to touch, to caress, to encompass.

"The condition," the director replied, "is that you also adopt two other children—"

Leon interrupted: "Absolutely out of the question. That's what I call nerve." Had he his way, they would have gotten up from their chairs and left St. Fernan, driven to Le Havre, and taken the next boat back to New York.

"Why does she insist on that?" Rose asked.

"The child says that the two children are close to her. They have wandered together in many cities. She says they are a work team."

"A work team?" Rose asked, puzzled.

"It's hard to explain. It's hard to imagine everything the children have experienced or what life has been like for them."

"No," Leon said adamantly. "I'm not going to be pushed into anything like that."

"Leon. Stop!" Her voice was a command. She turned to the director. "Please ask her if she will change her mind."

He spoke softly. The child shook her head vigorously.

"Leon," she pleaded, her cheeks trembling, "please, after what we have been through, after waiting so long. Please, in the few good years we have in front of us."

"Rosie, darling," his voice was a desperate entreaty. "We're not young anymore. We're almost sixty. It's crazy what you're asking me to do."

"Please."

In the corners of her eyes tears formed.

"All right. Just one more. Let her choose one more. Tell her," he said sharply to the director.

They watched the child listen to the translation. Expressionless. She paused, her brows slightly knitted. Placing her hands on her hips, the child nodded and said: "Naomi."

The director told the child to go look for and return with her companion, Naomi.

"You're very generous people," he said.

"We're crazy," Leon answered. He placed a hand on his wife's cheek. "Are you happy, Rosie?"

"No. No, I'm not happy. We should want to do everything to make the child happy. If she has two close friends that mean so much to her, why should we impose our will on her? Why? We can't afford it? We're giving a million dollars a year, at least, to charities where we don't even know the people who benefit. Why not to children who have been through so much? Oh, Leon, I'm not happy at all."

"My god," he sighed. "Isn't it going to be hard enough for people our age with two? Do we really need a third?"

She didn't answer. Her hands were pressed to her face.

"All right!" He jerked his chin at the director. "Who's the third?"

"By coincidence," said the director, "it's a little boy. Michel. He's about seven. I began telling you about him before. Ida Kaminets thinks he's a particularly sensitive and intelligent child."

"A boy?"

"Yes."

"Rosie? You hear, the third one in the business deal is a boy. It won't be so bad, two girls and a boy. Is that all right with you?"

Rose Howard was beaming.

Chapter 7

RELOCATIONS

Mowiss had requested the assignment at the Mittersill camp to give himself one last chance to practice medicine. The last year had been stultifying: with a lone noncommissioned officer and seven clerks, he tried to determine the cause of death of skeletons that reportedly were those of Americans "missing in action." It was neither administration nor medicine. It was plain busy work, dull and repetitive, and while it helped get the stench of Birkenau out of his nostrils the monotony of the work was unending. He left as early as possible each day to find a woman to spend the night with. Mittersill, if nothing else, offered some variety. He had been warned by his predecessor of the festering sores on the buttocks of the retarded children. A connection between intelligence and buttock infection? The main problem at the DP centers, he was informed, would be the political squabbles between administrators and inmate groups but, fortunately, he could stay clear of these daily eruptions and stick to medical rounds.

At Mittersill he had more time to himself than he had anticipated. In the adult barracks there were, among the inmates, men and women who, years earlier, had been doctors or nurses. His time was spent in the barracks with younger men and women who, except for an occasional emergency, were in pretty good condition, and with the children.

They walked, hobbled, or sat looking blankly ahead, a tag pinned to their clothing over the right breast. Mainly administrative information. Date of release from a previous camp, date of transfer into a military zone, date of entry into the camp at Mittersill. The space for family name was, for the children, blank or filled in with a stroke of ink; the space for given name repeated the name found on a similar tag from the previous camp.

A special clinic was organized for the youngest children, who were most vulnerable to communicable diseases. It was preventive rather than therapeutic, and it filled the day.

The smallest, frailest of the children, the one he had bet the medic would come down first with measles or chicken pox, was first on line every day of the special clinic for the first months. Whatever the weather, and even when a sudden surgery was required for an inmate in another barracks that kept the children waiting for hours, the boy with the tag on which was printed the name "Manfred" was there ahead of all the others.

"Okay, chum," he said patting the head, "Open your mouth and let's see if I won my bet. Ah, good. Nothing."

As the children left he noticed the boy remained behind. And when he walked to the parking lot on the other side of the high fence, the boy trailed him as far as the sentry's post.

After a while he found that as long as he held clinic or made rounds in the children's section of the camp, the child was never more than a few feet away.

"Hey! Manfred's a heavy name for a little nothing of a shrimp like you. The Russians turned you over to us, let's make believe you're a Slav! Mishka, come here."

For the first time in the months since he arrived at Mittersill a smile appeared on the child's face. He slowly approached until he stood by Mowiss's side, like a hound awaiting a command. Then he sat on a tree stump in front of the infirmary.

"You flea-bitten scruff of nothing, c'mere," he said pulling the child on to his lap. The large eyes sunk into sallow cheeks stared at him. "You're Darwin's proof. You've made it through the tenth plague. Here." He peeled the wrapper from a stick of chewing gum and daubed the boy's lips with the powdery sugar coating. The boy's bony fist pressed the stick into his mouth. "Chew gum, chum!"

The lean body pressed into his chest; a bending, arching motion of the spine pulled Mowiss's arm more tightly, protectively around him.

"The continent stinks of death and perversion. Nothing's happened, everything's happened. Lots of blood, hunks of flesh, a dissecting table three thousand miles wide. What am I? A bucket boy emptying bowels on the Elysian fields. What are you, little chum? A fluke. How the hell did you make it? Go ahead, sleep." He rested his chin gently on the boy's head as the swollen, bluish lids closed and the boy breathed almost inaudibly.

Mowiss began to whisper: "Suppose I take you back with me? Suppose? I'll pretend to be a widower, scrub you up, get you a stepmother, send you to medical school, prepare you for the next slaughter, the next plague. When I run out of pills or I'm too blotto to stick myself, you'll do or what's a son for? No, I'm a killer. Maybe you have the seed that'll survive the jungle. I'll buy stock in it, my hedge against the inflation of the egos that are choking us. It's a long-shot. Here!" Leaning to one side so as not to jostle and wake the child, he reached into the pocket of his coat, removed five silvery coins, tossed them onto the muddy ground, and buried them with a grinding of the heel of his boot. "A deal's a deal. Live, you little son of a bitch!"

Contrary to camp rules, Dr. Mowiss allowed two agents from a Jewish organization to enter the barracks. The camp would be shut down in a matter of weeks. Word had already been received from the zone commandant. Rules no longer had any force, or could be overlooked without repercussions. He agreed to let them designate ten boys to be circumcised. With luck they would be transferred to a holding camp, pending high-level governmental discussions and decisions about the countries to which Jews would be repatriated. With luck they would be transferred to what would eventually become the nation of Israel.

No stickler for rules in the battlefield operating tents, he was even less mindful of them in the last days of the DP camp. By the time a countermand could be delivered, the mud would have been turned into a potato field and he would be gone. He performed a few desultory tasks, including brief unemotional good-byes to the women he had lived with during the year as medical officer of the camp: the Austrian singer, the widow of the Dutch museum curator whom he feared was afflicted with cancer. He knew he would never see them again or even remember them for very long.

The youngest ten were chosen; all had dark hair and frightened eyes. The youngest and frailest was the child he had affectionately called Mishka. He had knobby elbows and knees and, tripping most of the time, followed Mowiss on his rounds of inspection. That night, ten ritual surgeries were performed. There was much pain and much restrained whimpering. A popular game in the camp among the staff and troops who performed guard duties involved guessing the national origin of the children by the shapes of their faces, gait, mannerisms. Among the adults there were Germans, Greeks, Italians, Russians, Bulgarians, Czechs, Finns, Spaniards, Hungarians, Rumanians, Dutch, French, even some Turks and Norwegians. But the children? No one knew. They spoke in monosyllables. Many languages—all in monosyllables.

Mishka followed Dr. Mowiss from barracks to barracks, often standing by his side as he treated cuts and bruises in the whitewashed infirmary. Mowiss always managed to have some chocolate or cigarettes to press into the child's thin hands.

He gave commands to the six-year-old. The boy understood and eagerly obeyed, but spoke little.

"You're tongue-tied, little fellow. Here's a piece of chocolate. Here, go smoke this cigarette."

The next morning, he said his good-byes to the English journalist he had lived with in the inn a few miles west of Mittersill. She would pack her small sack, tie it onto the frame of her bicycle and ride the few miles to the French

Zone. It took only an hour from the camp. They agreed to wave if they saw each other as the road to the French Zone passed by the camp.

Beads of rain clung to the barbed wire that surrounded the camp. He entered. A strange air of desolateness and quiet prevailed. The first barracks were empty. In the second were a small group of elderly men smoking, wheezing, cursing their fate. He bit his lips. The barracks with the youngest children was empty. A political settlement had been made and the procedures for repatriation speeded up, he was told. Gone. Here and there the seriously maimed and defective children leaned against the sides of the white building scratching imagined vermin from their bodies. A few blind children groped in the alleys between the wooden buildings. Some bit the flesh from their fingers or beat their heads rhythmically against the side of the barracks. Rejected merchandise. There was no flap of skin that could be readily severed with a deft cut of a scalpel that qualified them for a political settlement of their problem. No surgical procedure could be used to make them Italian, Bulgarian, Protestant, or Catholic. He doled out the chocolates and cigarettes he had brought for Mishka. They grasped at his hands greedily.

The scent of the Englishwoman lingered. She left, as a souvenir of their weeks together, a photograph and a dainty handkerchief with embroidery in a corner. Although Spring was close, it was still damp, still cold. He lighted a fire in the heavy iron stove that stood in the far end of the room and wrote two letters. The first was addressed to the commanding officer of the sector medical corps requesting after closing the camp, to spend the rest of the year in Paris before resigning his commission after nearly six years of service, more than five of them in the European theater of operations and so forth and so forth.

The second letter was addressed to his investment broker in New York. He indicated he would be back by the end of the year, that while he had not counted, five years of Captain's pay sent directly to him from the army paymaster's office must now add up to quite a bundle along with the many thousands of dollars he had sent directly to him from his financial activities while serving in Europe:

payments for instant VD cures for colonels and generals, payments for abortions performed on uniformed and civilian women employees of the military, payments for antiritual surgery, payments to cover up and comfort severe symptoms of alcoholic psychosis among visiting congressmen and senators, and payments for services whose nature was forgotten the moment they were paid for.

The instructions to the broker were to buy a lucrative retainership in an insurance company, shares in newly organized companies set up to buy victory ships, fractional parterships in highrise office buildings that were sure to be built before 1950.

He would turn fifty-three in December. Too late to renew a full practice, too late to follow the tracks of specialists grown fat and rich over the past six years. Make money. Lots of money and for no purpose in particular. If the only rule is madness, then money is the rule of rules. No backbreaking housecalls, hospital rounds, emergencies. Medicine is for the birds. A way to keep bodies alive, bodies that don't deserve life. There is no cure for mankind's disease—the madness that he had helped sow over Europe's vast dissecting table. Human quartersections dumped into hastily carved trenches while their owners looked on howling in pain and horror, bleeding stumps stacked in the corner of the tent because the medic's arm was blown off from a mine and was waiting on a litter, eyeballs thrown into the bloodsoaked fields and seized by ravenous crows, syphillis as rampant as athlete's foot, murderers glorified, the weak and feeble-minded turned insane from hunger nibbling at the bark of trees. In the first weeks after the guns were silenced, he had treated more human bite wounds, certified more strangulated corpses than in the twenty years of practice before enlisting. Medicine? Dross. Only money. Money to buy the sharpest scalpel to carve out the nonmalignant cancer that consumed him.

In a month all the paperwork was completed. The remaining days were uniform: medical examinations for departing refugees and the usual cuts and bruises, sore throats, cramps, fainting, and the unpredictable sequellae of severe emotional trauma and malnutrition. The deaf-mutes, mongoloids, cretins, and cripples of all ages and nationalities were not wanted back in the lands from whence they came. They would be shipped to religious homes in Australia and South America. Many others were merely being shipped from one occupation zone to another because the political settlement required this. One day the soldiers departed. Another day the camp administrators carried their duffel bags to waiting trucks and departed. As requested by the commanding officer of the zone medical corps in response to his request to spend the remainder of his service in Paris, he stayed in the camp until the last civilian employee departed. The few trees in the vicinity blossomed, the ground turned green, the air felt warm.

He requisitioned a prewar four-door Peugeot, enough fuel authorizations to last a year, put on the lightweight tan tunic, and drove to Paris. Wine was abundant and good, the bread coarse and indigestible; white bread could only be bought once a week on the black market.

There was an abundance, too, of pretty women from many capitals, either single and eager to land an American officer, or divorcees—bitter, disappointed, overly political, and burning with a sense of mission to solve the wretched refugee problem. After a few weeks in Paris he met one such divorcee at an outdoor café and they became steady companions, spending alternate nights together in their respective hotel rooms.

She was on the staff of one of the UN's numerous refugee committees. She monitored and coordinated with French and American occupying authorities the inter-zone transfer of groups numbering more than ten refugees. Up to ten refugees could cross borders without complications; more than that number subjected the group to regulations promulgated by the occupying authorities, the UN, and governmental advisory commissions. Her job was to determine whether a refugee group sought temporary residence in one of the shelters run by a political or religious organization which had been approved by the UN, or whether it wished to apply for special status subject to repatriation policies, which meant it could gain time while it waited to see which country would be most hospitable and raise the fewest questions regarding its origins. Periodically she was called upon to inspect a shelter in France and she welcomed the opportunity, since it allowed her to spend a few weeks in Paris.

She apparently was Dutch. During the days when she was busy, Mowiss bought large quantities of black-market antiques and shipped them to his broker in New York. He loaned money to fellow officers who wanted to buy stolen Army vehicles; the loans were repaid at a rate of interest equaling the principal. Perhaps the hotel clerks spread the word about his activities, for wherever he strolled Americans always asked to speak with him for a few minutes. Stranded ex-GIs, short of money who, for a little cash, could acquire a case of silk stockings selling for ten dollars a pair; some were Army deserters who simply wanted a handout to finance forged documents and passage back home.

On a day in July Dr. Mowiss sat at the table of an outdoor café and read the latest report from his broker. Arrangements for the future seemed bright. In addition to the insurance practice, there was a contract to franchise physicians as doctors for chains of theaters, for fire departments, and sporting events. The arrangements cost a good deal, but repaid handsomely. A woman slid into a wicker chair beside him. She was short, her hair prematurely gray and cut like a man's. Her high, protruding cheekbones made her eyes appear unusually intense.

"You are Dr. Mowiss?"

"Yes." She was no more than fifty-two, about his own age, he thought, but not pretty. Too short and dumpy. He offered her a drink from the bottle of white wine that stood on the small round table. She shook her head.

"You have worked in the camps with children, I know."

"Uh-huh."

"I heard of many fine things you have done."

Her strongly accented sounded Central European. It was an assertive voice with a rasping quality.

He smiled.

"I did what had to be done," he said. "On a beautiful summer day like today I try to convince myself that someday there will be no more war, no more killing. No more children carted around like political merchandise."

"That may be true. Let us pray for it. But I am concerned with what we can do now. I want your help." Her gaze was like a scalpel. This was no sly black marketeer and clearly no street frump eager to open her thighs for a month's supply of Wrigley's spearmint chewing gum.

"How can I help you?"

"In your car. I'll direct you."

It was a two-hour drive over the flat plains to the south and west of the grim capital. After the railroad yards, the coal depots, the grimy factories, the flat land yielded to lush, green rolling meadows and pastures. They passed villages where stone buildings looked as if giant mechanical creatures had bitten away chunks of wall. Farmers sweated in the field and swore at tired old animals. The heads of wheat were not yet yellow; beet greens looked young and pale. The puny beef cattle had just begun to adjust to new surroundings. During the last six months of the war nearly one and a half million cows, bulls, heifers and calves disappeared from the soil of France. The woman directed Mowiss to turn right at the stone marker beyond the village of La Barre. The main road became a single-lane path barely wide enough for the Peugeot. They reached the hamlet of St. Fernan and drove another mile uphill until the path leveled onto a broad verdant plateau. They stopped at a large gray manor house and about sixty wooden barracks. Thousands of children romped in the grass or seemed to be asleep on blankets spread under chestnut trees. Most were smiling. Dozens ran up to the car to greet the driver and his female passenger. He drove slowly on toward the manor house.

"What's your name?"

"It makes no difference. We are here."

"What is this place?" Mowiss asked.

"A DP camp, yet not a DP camp. The food is decent, but never enough. But there are no fences. The children have hope. There is no need for fences to enclose them like animals or prisoners. Over there is a school. Two to three hours a day of lessons. English, French, Hebrew.

Languages mostly. This place represents a tremendous victory won by the Jewish community of France. While the fights for jurisdiction continue here they have security; here they are under the jurisdiction not of the French government who didn't want them—but of the Jews of France. There are five thousand children here, all under fourteen. They survived the concentration camps and the DP camps. They were saved from political discussions and political betrayal. Records turned up nothing about who they are or where they come from. Nobody claims them, that is, they are claimed only by Jews. The children are now all Jews. They are the joyous responsibility of all Jewry. Some will be sent to the Jewish community of Canada. A few hundred. Some, a handful, will be sent to Jewish families in Cuba. Some, thousands I pray, will someday go to Palestine. When? God only knows. Your American government will allow in only a few hundred a month from DP camps, but none—none from this one, for it is officially under French jurisdiction. Go and explain to your government that France has denied jurisdiction. The children are stateless. The fortunate ones will go to America only from camps in Austria."

"What do you want from me?"

"I have families in New York, Boston, Chicago—families in many cities of America that want to adopt children. They long to have children of their own. They are prepared to adopt these." Her hands made a sweeping gesture toward the warm, sunny fields. "But it's all very illegal and the penalties are very severe, but the officials at the border in France and in America are sympathetic and willing to overlook things. I bring families here. They pick. They adopt. The officials are not too fussy about false papers, especially when there are not too many at one time. It costs, though. But the price is reasonable. It's worth it."

"I agree," Mowiss said softly.

"Tomorrow, I go to America. To New York. I have reservations on a boat from Le Havre. In five days I will see people in New York and tell them children for them are here. I will be back here in a few months. There will be two, maybe five families coming back with me. I need your money for documents, for the officials, for reaching many more families, for help to keep this place filled with sunshine and hope."

"Back at my hotel," Mowiss said. "I won't disappoint you. Shall we start?"

They walked back to the car along a gravel path. A clattering of stones and a high-pitched voice trailed from behind.

"Monsieur, monsieur, c'est moi-Mishka. Ton Mishka." A slightly built boy ran toward them.

They turned. The boy ran up to Dr. Mowiss and locked his hands around the man's knees. He recognized his favorite from the camp in Austria.

"Mishka!" he shouted, pulling the child into his arms and raising him over his head. "My little cigarette puffing chum. My sweet little old tongue-tied ragamuffin pal. I'll be damned! So you wound up here?"

The woman with the gray short-cropped hair restrained a smile.

"What is the chance," he asked, "that this little bumpkin can be sent to America?"

"It can be arranged, but it takes time. There is no guarantee. So many things can happen. People who come here to adopt a child usually have some special reason in their hearts. Most want newborns and there are none. You cannot know for sure."

"I understand," he said, frowning. He placed the boy on the ground and planted a kiss on his forehead. "Is it all right to give him something?"

"Better not. Everyone here has only what is genuinely needed."

Mowiss gave the child an affectionate slap on the behind and the child scampered off toward the fields.

"If the kid comes to America," he asked, "I would like to know where I can reach him and for him to know where he can reach me. I presume you would know how to arrange that?"

She nodded.

They returned to Paris. During the drive he mentioned a couple he once knew whom he had promised to help adopt a child.

Chapter 8

DEPARTURES

So much of each day was the same. Cassie woke them with a playful tug on the ear, hurried them to wash, handed them the clothing they were to wear, served them breakfast, escorted them downstairs to the sleek limousine where Leon's chauffeur drove them to school, picked them up at the end of the day, and delivered them home. Cassie served them dinner after they finished their school assignments, over which they were assisted every day by one or more tutors, and saw to it that they were in bed at the time Rose Howard indicated. They saw their parents at dinnertime on Friday night, birthday festivities, school ceremonies, on the days they left for summer camp and on their return. Rose and Leon Howard had few conversations with the children; talk with them consisted mainly of questions and compliments. Rarely did either of them command the children to do anything; this was left to the principal at Hartley, their teachers, tutors, their elevator operator and doorman, the chauffeur, and Cassie. Saturdays were devoted to appointments with doctors, dentists, dancing lessons, coaching to rid their speech of clumsy foreign accents, and visits with classmates either in their own home or, if in the home of another child, with prior approval by Rose Howard. Sundays were spent in recreation groups in which they were enrolled by their mother. When they were alone it was usually to watch a program on television; their argument about who would decide what to watch brought Cassie running. After a few months of argument, Leon gave each a personal set and they joined together after trying different programs on their own sets and settling on the best one. There were not many occasions when they visited alone with classmates or received them at home. Throughout the school year, there was a birthday party held about once a week. Each party was the same. A master of ceremonies who talked, sang, organized dancing, told them when to eat, when to play pin-the-tail-on-the-donkey, to sing "Happy Birthday" when the cake was brought out by a Negro housekeeper, and when to dress to wait in the downstairs corridor for a maid, a governess, or chauffeur to take them home. Naomi made rapid progress in English and performed in class, by the end of her first year at Hartley, with the brighter students. Michael learned English even more rapidly and, because he could outrun most of the boys in his class, was liked by his classmates and esteemed by them, although not by his teachers, as the smartest kid in the class. It took a long time for Deborah to speak English passably; her accent thickened rather than diminished. The report that Rose and Leon Howard received from her psychoanalyst indicated that her apparent lack of interest in school, poor grades, tendency to periodically overeat, and avoidance of friendship might be due to a glandular problem and/or anxiety. When they got the report, they arranged for Deborah to have a checkup by the chief of endocrinology at Mt. Sinai Hospital. He assured them that Deborah's glands were normal and that while he knew and respected the psychoanalyst who had written the report, he couldn't understand why she thought it might be a glandular problem. The analyst met with Deborah twice a week for the rest of the year, but it did not help Deborah win friends or improve her schoolwork. After summer camp, the Howards decided to send both daughters to different psychoanalysts. Michael usually refused to visit doctors, dentists, or the psychoanalyst—that is, except for Dr. Mowiss.

Michael was eleven when he went to Mowiss for the first time. He had argued with his drama teacher.

"Everyone in the class must have a part in the Thanksgiving play. Your father and mother will be coming and you must be one of the Pilgrims," the teacher said imperiously.

"I won't. I won't." He thought of the silly plays where Naomi tried to disguise her accent, where Deborah never opened her mouth except to sing with the chorus. "I won't!" he shouted, his body stiff with fury.

"Then," the teacher replied, embarrassing him in front of his classmates, who tittered, "I'm sending you home."

He waited in the office while the secretary spoke to Cassie. The chauffeur would pick him up as soon as possible.

When the secretary stepped away from the office, he found the address in the telephone directory and quickly left the school building. Michael went to Dr. Mowiss, walking from the school on East Seventy-Fourth, off Madison, to Thirtieth and Park.

Dr. Mowiss was alone in the office. He never received patients; that was not the kind of medicine he practiced. He was on call to insurance companies and hotels; the generous retainers arrived regularly whether or not he made calls and performed examinations. There were special fees for each examination and by referring most patients to specialists, the split fee added to his income. The money rolled in and he didn't get entangled in the petty politics of hospitals; he also preferred not to waste his time on hospital calls. He had already been able to increase to ten percent his holdings in the new twenty-story hotel in downtown Philadelphia; to a twentieth interest in a Panamanian cargo fleet he had also bought on speculation, a thousand-acre turkey farm in North Carolina, and a twenty-room house in the Hamptons. All without having to torment himself about whether his diagnosis was accurate or not. Any jerk fresh out of medical school could handle nine out of ten complaints. The other ten percent were incurable, anyhow. Referring most cases to specialists relieved him of the headaches.

"Mishka," he exclaimed with genuine pleasure when Michael entered. "My little Mishka. Come on and give your American uncle a big kiss."

Michael leaped into the widespread arms and burst into sobs.

Mowiss hugged him, kissed the wet cheeks, and hummed a tune to the child as he waited for the sobbing to subside. "For pete's sakes, a boy almost eleven years old crying like a nine-year-old. Come on, old fellow, cheer up." He playfully boxed the child's ears. The tears turned to laughter.

"Do your mother and father know you're here?"

The slender forehead creased. "They're not my mother and father."

"Okay, sport. Have it your way. Do Mr. and Mrs. Howard, your adoptive parents, know your whereabouts?"

Michael shook his head.

"You are, therefore, a runaway. That's a crime. The law can stack you away for years and years and years; you'll be so old when they let you out you'll have a white beard down to your ankles."

The child laughed.

"Why did you run away, you brigand, you Sicilian outlaw, you thief of parents' tranquility? What for?"

Michael shrugged.

"I'll call them right now so they don't worry." Mowiss reached for the telephone.

Michael grasped his hand. "No!" he shouted.

"Okay, sport. I won't. They'll have conniptions. But have it your way. What can I do for you?"

Silence.

"You want a heart-to-heart man-to-man talk?"

Silence.

"You want a checkup, maybe?"

"Yes," Michael answered, stiffening as if he actually had been reluctant to confess a secret ailment.

"Very well, sit. Where does it hurt?"

Michael pointed to his heart.

"Heart condition? Very well." He picked up the stethoscope from his dusty desktop, placed the prongs in his ears, and the silver disc against the boy's chest, asking him to breathe deeply.

"My, my my! The familiar heartbeat of a centaur. You shall live a thousand years, my little creature."

"What's that?"

"A centaur?"

"Yes."

"An imaginary beast with extraordinary powers and a long life. But half-man, half-beast. Poor duff, he doesn't quite know who or what he is. Like you little chum."

Michael sat in the doctor's lap and for a few minutes neither said anything.

"Let me call your home. They'll surely have apoplexy."

"No," Michael said, his narrow lips tightening. "If you do, I'll never want to see you ever again. Promise you won't tell them."

"You're making me a conspirator, old chap. They'll have us both behind bars for a million years, if we enter into such a diabolical compact."

"Promise me."

"Okay, I promise."

"Inside my head," the child began, "sometimes, every day, I do terrible things."

"Like?"

"Like I kill soldiers and men and women."

"Do you kill little animals? Dogs? Kittens? Rabbits?"

"No, just people. Soldiers."

"Inside your head it's okay. Some people don't even have the advantage of having that inside their heads and they go ahead and do it anyhow."

"I don't like where I am."

"Did you like the camp in St. Fernan better?"

"No. I hated it there."

"Where would you rather be?"

"With you."

"That's beautiful, old sport." Mowiss kissed the child's forehead. "But it's not in the cards. I tell you, whenever you want to come and stay a bit with your American uncle, you come right ahead and we'll keep the deal quiet, a secret—I promise." Michael stayed for three days. The two of them went to restaurants together. They shopped to buy nightclothes for Michael as well as a tooth brush and a few books.

"Where were you?" Rose pleaded, restraining both her anger and the hand that would have lashed out to strike him. Leon had left the office as soon as she called. They thought about kidnapping, but there were no indications of this: no letters, no calls; the detective who had come from the precinct said there were absolutely no signs of kidnapping; he would discount that possibility. More likely, he speculated, the boy had simply run away.

"They turn up in a few days." He cited statistics about the number of runaway boys and girls.

They took medicine to calm themselves. Deborah and Naomi went from school to their various lessons, dutifully practiced their musical instruments, prepared their homework neatly, bathed, watched family comedies on the television, and went quietly to sleep. To their questions about Michael, Leon and Rose impatiently told them they didn't know, but were confident he would be found.

Chapter 9

MICHAEL

At the end of the freshman high school year at Hartley, Michael was the top-ranking student in all subjects except one—physical education. He did not share the exaggerated enthusiasm of the other boys for basketball or swimming. As much as he could, without invoking snide remarks by the physical-education instructor, a graduate history student from Columbia, he avoided tennis, riding; even Ping Pong left him with a feeling of chilled disinterest. He had reached full height, was underweight, slim, got no particular satisfaction from flexing his biceps in front of the mirror. He had begun to shave the soft fuzz on his cheeks and upper lip, and went about, like the other boys, with shirtsleeves rolled to expose hairy forearms. He was no bookworm, his grades were outstanding without effort, although he dated girls from Hartley and the posh all-girl schools on the East Side. He derived as much pleasure from spending Saturday night at Dr. Mowiss's playing chess.

Occasionally, Jean, Mowiss's first wife, joined them.

The summer camp Leon and Rose selected was a work camp for boys, an expensive camp located in the White Mountains of New Hampshire. Campers built roads, log cabins, rail bridges over streams. The directors of the camp assured Leon and Rose that they would see to it that Michael was encouraged to develop a more active interest in sports.

Assigned to work crews with five other boys and a counselor, Michael began each day's labors by designing techniques calling for a minimum expenditure of physical effort. "Why the hell should we carry logs like some goddamn ignorant Egyptian slave when they can be rolled on other logs?" Michael chided them. "Why in hell do we have to chop down trees with a goddamn boy-scout ax when there's a chain saw in the toolshed?" The others agreed and their constructions were undertaken with little effort, affording them unscheduled time for leisurely canoe trips on the nearby lakes and streams, langorous days in the woods listening to the sounds of birds and crickets, or reading. It had become wearisome and Michael longed to see Dr. Mowiss. He left a note for the camp director: "Please tell my parents not to worry. I've gone on a little trip. Will be back home by Labor Day."

Leon and Rose chartered a plane and flew to the New Hampshire camp. Neither the sheriff or the local police had had any idea of Michael's whereabouts. The camp director stammered with embarrassment. For three days the guest cottage on the camp grounds was turned into a search headquarters. Forest rangers reported that they had identified all campers and hikers, but Michael was not among them. The sheriff advised Leon and Rose to accept the message at face value and not to worry. After all, he was fifteen and could handle himself. If there were a problem, they would certainly hear.

They packed Michael's things and shipped them back to New York.

"Why?" Rose asked plaintively.

"Why, anything?" Leon replied helplessly. He wanted to swear, but couldn't find the words.

Through Dr. Mowiss's answering service, Michael found out that Mowiss was registered in a Reno, Nevada, hotel. He hitchhiked from the New Hampshire town to Albany where he boarded a Greyhound bus to Reno.

"Mishka! my beloved wandering comrade," Dr.

Mowiss exclaimed, embracing the boy with a bearlike hug. "Like old times. Why?"

"I wanted so much to see you."

"Of course. No need to expound. Let's get away from this incubator of adultery and twenty-four-hour roulette and live a bit. You got me on the threshold of checking out. Let's go!"

"The camp wasn't bad. I guess it was okay. But I just didn't get any satisfaction from anything."

The car was headed toward California. The sun blazed; the crystalline desert sparkled an intense heat and light.

"The beginning of the world is here. Creation! Nothing but barrenness. Our own lives until . . . unless it is transformed. But only at a great price. What are you willing to pay, my man?"

"For what?"

Dr. Mowiss laughed. He cursed the dry heat that penetrated the sealed car.

"Rented cars! Ugh! The air conditioning is lousy."

"Pay for what?" Michael repeated.

"For wisdom, my lad. Wisdom. For a taste of life and true understanding."

"I've got about sixteen dollars left."

"A deal. Sealed in blood. Hold onto it. I trust you. You will have wisdom on a credit card. I suppose you didn't tell your parents?"

"I left them a note," he said shyly.

"Better than nothing. Let's zoom across this godforsaken emptiness." The setting sun set the desert ablaze, producing an inferno of color.

On the Pacific, midway between Los Angeles and San Diego, Mowiss rented a beach house; its marble terrace faced the ocean. Together they bought food, swimming trunks, and books to read in the evening. Except for eating and sleeping they spent the first three days on the warm, golden sand or trying to ride the surf into shore. The eternal crests permitted only intermittent swimming.

On the fourth day, Dr. Mowiss said, "Mishka, my lad, I am in dire need of female companionship and so I'm driving up to Hollywood and will be gone for two or three days. Here is some cash to attend to your needs until I get back. And I suggest you befriend that charming young thing in the bookstore at the shopping center." He got into the car and drove away. For several hours Michael sat on the marble terrace listening to the grind of the ocean, watching the furtive maneuvering of the gray gulls. He repeated to himself the long conversations he had had with Dr. Mowiss at night before they went to sleep.

"That bit of foreskin I lopped off your infantile member made you Jewish, but only in the most important and the same time insignificant sense. Important because it established a physical label and in the primitive, irrational state of mankind's thinking, those labels are paramount. Insignificant because one fiftieth of a gram of epidermis is not sufficient flesh to affect consciousness, awareness, or consecration. Do you feel Jewish?"

"For a while, just during the Bar Mitzvah they made me have, I felt it."

"At precisely what juncture?"

"I think it was when I had to carry the Torah. It was like suddenly I belonged somewhere, fit in somewhere. And when they were talking about 'our people': Abraham and Isaac and Moses and Jacob, for a while I felt that they were really my ancestors."

"And . . . ?"

"And then I felt it wasn't so at all. I don't have any relatives. I mean not really knowing, the cave men or the apes could just as well be my real ancestors or for that matter anything or anybody. You know that."

"Indeed, indeed. I have been trying to put a soul into your corporeal shell, but it will take time."

"How?"

"By giving you the gift of solitude. That's the sole and exclusive reason for my taking part in this conspiracy of flight. Solitude! You can't fill, convert, or transform that bloody thing, my man. It wears you like a lion skin. When you wear it, you'll be home free."

They were interrupted by numerous telephone calls from New York. The three-hour difference in time meant that New York offices had just closed and Mowiss's brokers could discuss the day's transactions and receive instructions for tomorrow's business. The one-sided talk was much like those he overheard at home by Leon's side. Buy, hold, sell, transfer, percentage, bind, deposit. The business of business. He went to his room to read and they didn't resume their conversation.

He put on a tee shirt, a pair of dungarees, and walked, barefoot, the several palm-lined streets to the bookstore in the shopping center.

Shirlianne was a sophomore at the University of California, working as a salesgirl, taking in as much sun and sea as she could, living by herself and measuring the success of her summer of freedom by the number of love affairs she could consummate. Since Michael had no notion of either seduction or rape, Shirlianne was a willing, artful instructor who did not mention either Michael's age (she was nineteen) or his inexperience. She moved in with him during Mowiss's absence and their amorous entanglements were a combination of gymnastic feats, delicate mutual temptations, and erotic explorations that fell just short of armed violence. Suddenly tutored, suddenly aware of senses undeveloped and the sheer easy pleasure that bodies give one another, he was grateful to his tanned companion, happy to be with her, but the joy he had discovered was mainly below the shoulders; he couldn't get rid of the brooding hornets of anger that rattled his brain.

"What are you?" Michael asked. They were lying nude, side by side, on the blue wall-to-wall carpet in the living room. Their hands and fingers were sticky and yellow from eating mangoes.

"I'm a girl, silly. See." She turned to one side and pointed to the signs of her femininity.

"I don't mean that," Michael said with annoyance. "I mean are you Catholic or Jewish or what?"

"I know that you're Jewish," she said teasingly. "I can tell, tra la la. . . ."

"I'm serious."

"But what difference does it make? We're all brothers and sisters under the skin. Religion is the opiate of the masses. Marx said that. We learned it in political science. I believe it. Can you imagine all the millions of people who have been exterminated since the dawn of civilization because of religion? Disgusting. I'm for social justice and equality. Down with national frontiers and passports." She stood up and pretended to be carrying a placard as she marched around the room.

"Quit it, will you. I'm serious. What are you?"

She folded her legs under her, sitting beside Michael.

"My father was a Catholic. He was killed during the war. I never knew him. Just pictures. Very handsome. My mother's Jewish. Not a gung-ho practitioner. Once-a-year Passover supper and that's it. She didn't remarry and now that she's getting a little lonely she's joining Jewish clubs and things like that. That answer your question?"

"Yes."

Until the day before Labor Day, Mowiss spent three or four days a week with Michael in the rented house and left him alone the rest of the time when he went to Hollywood. When Mowiss was absent, Shirlianne lived with Michael. On the eve of her return to Los Angeles, they spent their last night together sleeping on the beach in the sand, wrapped in blankets under the overhanging terrace. They did not mention seeing each other again and neither asked for the other's address.

The next day Mowiss entered with a pretty brunette.

"Mishka, old comrade. I would like to present my dearest, newest friend, Eloise Brent, née Braunschwieg. Meet Michael Howard, né everyman." A polite handshake.

Michael gaped, in part at the surprise return and in part at the striking beauty of Mowiss's new companion. And for the first time, he felt naked standing in front of a mature woman. His face colored deeply.

"We're going to perform a ritual celebration of our friendship right here in this enchanted hideaway. I'll probably be here through Thanksgiving if you want to write or call. I've gotten myself into making a movie—with Eloise in an important part. Here is a ticket back to New York, old chum. Good-bye. Blessings on all your endeavors."

"Where were you, Michael?" Leon asked. His anger had long since cooled and he was actually pleased to see the boy look so well, tanned, poised and, perhaps, as he would have liked to believe, more muscular.

"California. The ocean."

"It's nice in California," Rose mused. Neither pressed further.

When autumn sighed its melancholy coolness into the city, the lives of Leon, Rose, and their three children resumed their organized rhythms. It was the second and final year at fashionable Clarendon for Naomi and Deborah; Michael entered the sophomore year at Hartley.

In 1959, when he was nineteen and a freshman at Swarthmore, Michael was absent toward the end of the first semester for almost four months. He spent the time with Dr. Mowiss traveling in Europe. Mowiss abandoned Eloise Brent née Braunschwieg in Madrid and after the loss of a staggering amount of money in his attempt to become a movie producer, he gave up the suite of luxurious rooms he maintained at the Parkside Hotel, where he had entertained visiting directors, actors, actresses and investors. During the four months, he and Michael had many dates together until he found the European woman he decided to marry. When he introduced Rosalia Toledano, a divorcee from a family that manufactured carburetors in Milan, Michael knew that he would have to return home, leaving Mowiss to his honeymoon and European business investments.

He spent the remainder of the year reading, half-heartedly accompanying Leon and Rose to Madison Avenue galleries to buy paintings, and spending time at Leon's side at his office on Third Avenue learning about real estate.

"After all, Michael," he said as accountants and building managers filed in for meetings, "you are going to have charge of this when I'm gone."

Michael enrolled in New York University for the fall term. His attendance was regular and he spent all of his spare time with Leon at the office. When he had no dates on Saturday or Sunday, he accompanied Leon on short trips outside of the city to size up possible land and construction deals. Michael was becoming versed in the art of real estate and construction transactions; although it was no source of excitement, he enjoyed meeting the people with whom Leon dealt, confirming his father's judgment. When he felt at odds with Leon, he said nothing. At the beginning of the school year in 1963, Michael disappeared again for almost an entire year. Out of consideration for Leon and Rose, he telephoned them three, sometimes four times a week to tell them he was well. His two sisters were by then married. He did not, however, disclose his whereabouts or even vaguely suggest that they visit him. They would have been shocked at what they found.

Mowiss and his wife Rosalia had bought an abandoned bank on the lower East Side of Manhattan. Preserving the stained-glass dome that filtered in soft light, they had built a floor of bedrooms in a circle beneath the dome. A double spiral staircase led from the bedrooms to the mosaic floors below. The rear area was converted into a massive living room, dining room, and kitchen. The public part of the building had been turned into a bar and studio. Rosalia painted minutely detailed oils in a genre that critics referred to as pop-porno. Mowiss sculpted the same themes, figures, and action from parts of abandoned automobiles, airplane surplus, and partially destroyed household appliances.

Michael occupied one of the bedrooms with Fay Buttonwood, who had been a classmate of his at NYU until they both decided to leave school for an indefinite period. Michael and Fay helped Mowiss and his wife Rosalia with their art and in a space, which used to be the loan department of the former bank, they built a loom and wove rugs, ties, skirts, and serapes. Michael let his beard grow and left it untrimmed. It was black and smooth. When they lost interest in weaving, Michael and Fay painted.

Leon and Rose would have been shocked by the living arrangments, the pop-porno art, the weaving; they would have been most shocked by Mowiss's ravings.

He stood on a high platform where he had just finished welding a bumper guard to an iron pole fashioned from a restaurant counter.

"The mark of Cain is upon us all. We cannot love and love cannot make us whole. We can only kill, killing only can make us one." He wore a black yarmulka on his head and the long, tasseled blue-and-white talith, the prayer shawl of the orthodox Jew. "The summit we attain by a voyage through perdition. But there can't be perdition whenever all is perdition. You understand the syllogism, Mishka?"

"Yes, Rabbi," Michael assented. Today Mowiss was a rabbi, yesterday a Roman Catholic priest, the day before a Russian Orthodox patriarch from Odessa. Tomorrow?

"Hey, skinny legs," Mowiss bellowed. "Hey, you genetic fallout from the loins of a wasp sprung from Plymouth, what do you think of this Brancusilike phallus reaching for eternal glory in the stars."

Fay smiled without turning her eyes from the loom.

"I like to see completed work. It's not finished. When it's finished, I'll give you my opinion."

"It'll never be finished," Mowiss roared. "To finish something is to condemn it to death. I will be a killer no more. I'll be an ender no more. What time is it?"

That's the way the episodes ended. He would ask the time. Return to the mosaic floor. Have a small bite to eat and allow himself to be helped to the bedroom where, as Michael held him, Rosalia gave the injection.

Chapter 10

MICHAEL

Michael had not planned to avoid the graduation ball his parents had arranged at the Plaza. For them it would be another episode, another of his disappearing acts. Unlike Naomi and Deborah, Michael had refused to continue psychoanalysis. For his sisters, the sessions with the analyst resembled ballet lessons, orthodonture, or visits to the hairdresser. Rose Howard said this is what is to be done and it was done without protest, with smiles. It was for their own good. Whatever good it accomplished Michael could not know, since his sisters talked about the sessions as if they were treatments for blemishes. Sometimes when telling him what they had done during the day, they couldn't remember whether they were coming from the analyst or the English tutor. Michael would have none of it. He refused to go to the psychoanalyst as vehemently as he refused to have his teeth straightened; he acquired no skill at musical instruments, for he adamantly refused to submit to lessons. Whatever the analyst learned about Michael from the sessions with his sisters or from conversations with his parents, the insights shed no light on his periodic disappearances.

The festive voices and recessional music grew dim. He walked hurriedly from the steep hill leading down toward the busy avenue, away from the university campus. He had tossed the black gown and cap on a folding chair near the furthest exit gate. Someone would find it; if lost, the deposit would take care of it. The foolish garment wouldn't cause trouble to anybody.

A yellow cab pulled to the curb in response to his wave. He gave the driver Mowiss's address on Thirtieth and Park Avenue South. It would be a forty-minute drive, at least if the traffic was not too heavy. Forty minutes to blame Leon and Rose and the life that they had organized for him. A life permitting no digression, no variation preventing him from fulfilling the phantasy that came to him every day as regularly as hunger pangs and sleepiness: killing Germans. He would put poison in their drinking water, bayonet large numbers of them at their work and play, dynamite entire towns and villages—blast them from the face of the earth. The phantasies included neither bloodshed nor screams of the wounded and dying. They were silent. He sat against the brown-cushioned seat and savored the vision. He did not respond to the driver's remarks about what a sunny day it was, whether he had gone to the graduation, that his own daughter had graduated from college the June before, that he hoped it wouldn't rain when he took his vacation.

Motors growled. The spring mud on the road flew into the air. The convoy drove for several hours and finally came to a complete stop. The roads were impassable. There were thousands—tens of thousands—of soldiers jamming the roads, many lying on the banks of the road looking tired, curious, or unhappy.

He was going at Rosalia's request. She feared that her husband would hurt himself or someone else by his strange behavior. The episodes lasted only an hour or two each day. Sometimes after Mowiss took the injection he was perfectly all right and she had no fear that he would take up a piece of iron and strike someone. He became sleepy and whispered to Michael, pulling him close to his face: "Listen, sport. I've been infected with your plague. We've switched, don't you see? But the river isn't wide enough or deep enough for us both. I'll be back. Stay. . . ."

When he left the cab and entered the old, dusty, and disordered office that had served Mowiss and Rosalia as a home since they gave up the converted bank building, he found Rosalia near the door, suitcases at her side.

"It's the end," she said sadly. "I'm leaving this afternoon. They took him to Bellevue. He took a pipe from the gas range and wanted to kill policemen. The psychiatrist says it's hopeless. They'll put him in a state hospital for the rest of his life. It's the end. I tried. You know how much I tried. One day he wants to die. The next he wants to start all over. With what, I don't know. I'm going back to Milan. Good-bye, Michael."

He lived in the ramshackle office for a month until he succeeded in getting Mowiss released to his custody. It had taken a great deal of money for legal fees, bribes to the arresting policemen, and payments to the hospital's employees, but the amount made barely a dent in his personal account of which neither Leon nor Rose knew anything. The income from his trust funds went there and the frequent cash gifts from Leon as well as the substantial income from his numerous real-estate investments and portfolio of blue-chip stocks. Michael had accumulated over eighty thousand dollars in the account.

He rented a car and they drove to a small hotel in the Catskills. They stayed there until the first snow fell in mid-November. At the beginning Mowiss spent most of the time in agony—the cramps in his stomach and the muscles of his arms and legs, and the endless sweating, prevented him from eating. He threw fits of violence and anger, but in his weakened condition he could do little more than writhe in bed or badger Michael to release him from captivity. As the weeks went by, the episodes lessened and lasted for what seemed afterward to be only fleeting moments. During the time, he never mentioned Rosalia. They took long walks in silence through the leafless woods. They talked.

"I once had a patient. He and his wife were past eighty. She died. He brooded. You know why? He had no one to argue with any more. You and I, Mike, old chum, we're a dialogue. A dialogue of contradiction. Light and dark. Ends and beginnings. What's finished and what hasn't yet been started. You should have let me rot away."

"Did you?"

"Did I what?"

"Did you let me rot away?"

"Then I believed. Not a hell of a lot. But there was at least a tiny peg to hang my hat on. Now I couldn't sell my corpse to a half-assed mentally defective intern for a cup of coffee. I went through everything I thought was important as if I were walking on a sack of puffed rice. Crunch. Wham! Sand. Crumbs. Except for that flea-bag office that never saw a patient, I've nothing. Smoke!"

"You're still a doctor."

"I've stopped believing. No one's worth healing. I'm not even a third-rate has-been Western Union messenger boy for the angel of death. I should have put my head in the oven and turned on the gas."

Michael scooped a handful of the light snow and tossed it in the air watching it flutter like fine ash.

"Why didn't you adopt me?"

Mowiss turned his head sharply to face Michael. For the first time in weeks the deep creases of agony in the sunken cheeks appeared less scarlike. The hanging lower lip quivered to shape a smile.

"It stinks here. There must be a dead porcupine. Let's go back. I'm tired."

Michael said, "If you'll accept, I spoke to Abraham Breen who owns the Mountainview Hotel. He's agreed to retain you for the winter season as a house physician. A few hundred dollars a week, a good room, meals, and charming companions on singles' weekends."

"Start again? We die and we start again. Okay. When do I start?"

"Tomorrow, if you want."

"I want. Let's pack, old chum."

"I need a favor," Michael stammered. "I don't have a draft exemption any more. I don't want to go to Vietnam and I don't want to run off to Canada or claim conscientious-objector status."

"A medical reason? Easy. I could see the possibilities of a serious whiplash injury. I made my first, late lamented fortune on whiplash injuries. God! if I had a dime for every doctor who swears that plaintiffs in negligence cases have whiplash injuries, I could buy the Mountainview Hotel. I was probably the world's heavyweight champion in whiplash injuries. Or you can have something simple like chronic myocarditis. Sooner or later we all fall in love with an imagined affliction. Choose."

"The carditis thing sounds fine."

"It's done. You're a civilian. Give me the papers and I'll mail the report to your draft board tomorrow."

When after an absence of five months, Michael returned to the Park Avenue apartment, Leon and Rose didn't mention the fact that Michael had not come to the graduation party in his honor. They were more upset that Deborah and her husband Sidney had separated. Deborah was in the hospital and Rose's phlebitis had become so painful that she needed a nurse during the day to help her move about. Neither showed disappointment or surprise when Michael informed them that he had bought a brownstone on West Ninety-Third Street.

"With that Buttonwood girl?" Leon asked.

Michael nodded.

"You love her?"

"Not enough to marry. We get along okay. But we're not talking marriage, as yet."

"As yet is a big if!"

"Marrying doesn't mean too much, you know."

"I know. I know. I also know what my feelings are about Christian girls," Leon said stiffly.

"Dad, let's not get into that."

"I won't get into *that*."

"Besides, I haven't seen her for months."

"She calls every day asking if we've seen you or how you are. 'Have you at least heard from him?' she asks. That's a tough one to answer. Have you heard from him? A laugh."

"Dad, please."

"Have it your own way. But you'll regret it if. . . ."

He didn't finish. Rose hobbled painfully into the room and announced that the hospital had called, saying that it had been necessary to abort Deborah's pregnancy.

"Are you coming with us, Michael, to see your sister?" Rose asked, placing a hand on Michael's cheek.

"Of course, Mother."

He helped her with her coat and let her lean on his arm as they went out. As they waited for their limousine, he looked into the face of this kind, elderly woman whom he loved without loving, for whom he felt tenderness without having shown affection. If she could only have been my mother, he thought.

Chapter 11

BIRTHDAYS

On October 7, a deliveryman from Koustakis's Flower Shop on Madison Avenue brought Deborah a long white, gilt-decorated box. The odor hung over the box and she knew roses were inside. Twenty-five American Beauties. Except for the orchid that Leon and Rose gave her before going out to the theater, she received no other flowers that day. It was the same every year on her official birthday. At the camp in France there was only one festivity during the year to celebrate the children's birthdays. Leon and Rose had originally chosen October 7 for both Deborah and Naomi, since that was the date of their arrival in America. But their classmates at Hartley teased them about the fact that two sisters who looked completely unalike had the same birthday. Then their parents decided to give Naomi a different, later birthday.

There was a card in the box of roses. *"Merde.* P.S. Since I can't join the party tonight, please join Fay and me at the usual place."

The card was signed Michel, the name he was given in the camp at St. Fernan.

The usual place was Benjie's Cafeteria on Essex Street a few buildings from the corner of Delancey. It was an unpretentious eating establishment, a hangout for aging anarchists, anarcho-syndicalists, Trotskyites, and a motley assortment of Balkan, Turkish, and Greek revolutionaries.

A vision of social justice haunted their dimming eyesight. Talk about the triumph of the revolution in many tongues compensated for Benjie's greasy fare. Benjie's was also the hangout for Ida Kaminets. Ida Kaminets was a graduate student of engineering in Buffalo when war broke out in Poland in 1939. When word reached her describing the circumstances of her family's forced relocation from Warsaw to a labor camp in Silesia, she abandoned her studies and decided to devote the remainder of her life to rescuing Jews from countries where they could not breathe freely.

Among the idealists in Benjie's dancing to keep warm the one foot that was not yet in the grave, Ida always raised modest funds to rescue a human being, make contact with cousins-in-the-spirit abroad who could help carry out her work. It was at Benjie's at periodic meetings with Michael, Deborah, and Naomi that she raised much larger sums of money for the more costly part of her work: bribing border police, paying transportation, providing living needs until the escapee could establish himself or herself. There were no fixed appointments with Ida Kaminets. The Howard children, alone and by chance together, frequented Benjie's, and if Ida was present they transacted their business.

"Happy birthday." Fay kissed her on the cheek.

"Thank you for the lovely flowers, Michel, they're beautiful." She pulled him to her broad bosom and kissed him fondly, European style, on both cheeks.

Michael opened a bottle of wine and they drank while nibbling rather stale sugar cookies that Benjie heaped on a surplus naval-hospital platter.

"You want to tell her, Fay?" Michael asked.

"Sure," Fay said eagerly. "Mike and I both think that you would approve a birthday present that isn't so personal."

Ida Kaminets slipped unobtrusively into the empty chair by the table. By long-standing agreement they avoided small talk. Ida squeezed Deborah's right hand. She responded by beaming: the sparkle of her eyes, her wide voluptuous smile, was like sunshine in Benjie's seedy haven. Her radiance drew the attention of the elderly Italians, most of whom talked about resurrecting Judge Thayer so that they could execute him for giving the death sentence to the two peddlers Sacco and Vanzetti.

"Instead of something personal," Fay continued, "since more jewelry would choke you, Mike and I are each giving Ida three thousand dollars in your name."

"How wonderful!," Deborah exclaimed, caressing Fay's blonde head. "Beautiful. Nothing could give me more pleasure."

Ida Kaminets removed an envelope from her pocketbook and handed it to Deborah. It contained four recent photographs. Each showed a family: mother, father, two or three children. Deborah looked at the pictures and heard Ida say: "From Rumania. All of them. With this birthday gift they will be in Vienna before the end of the year."

"From there?" Deborah asked.

"Argentina, maybe. They would like Australia where they have cousins. That's the least problem."

"Thank you, Ida, for making it possible. I wish I could do more, but. . . ."

"Happy Birthday to you!" Michael began to sing. The revolutionists joined in. Benjie came out from behind the counter and wiped one hand on a soiled, tattered apron. He carried a cupcake with a single lighted candle.

The ballroom of the Plaza Hotel, even for the annual presentation of debutantes, was rarely as festively decorated. Wedding receptions for five hundred guests and two orchestras cost less. Leon had ordered three orchestras. At the four corners of the vast ballroom, four mermaids, sculpted from ice, seemingly suspended over gargantuan silver scallop shells, shimmered as bubbles of pink champagne cascaded off their transparent bodies. One thousand guests. Michael's friends and their families, his classmates going back to second grade and their families, his companions at the various summer camps and their families, and more than a hundred students of the graduating class of 1964 were invited. All in honor of Michael's graduation from New York University. Neither Leon or Rose danced; Leon because of the shortness of breath and the tightness in his chest. Rose because of the phlebitis that caused a painful but not noticeable swelling. They strutted proudly among the guests, assuring them that Michael was simply delayed and would soon arrive. They lied courageously. In fact they had no idea where Michael was, not having seen him since he walked sullenly away from them after the recessional march when all the other newly invested baccalaurates raced, black-gowned, into the waiting arms of parents and sweethearts. He disappeared into the throng.

Her face flushed, Naomi left the dance floor holding her husband's hand. Although only in the fourth month of pregnancy, the baby was more noticeable than her two previous children, both girls. Leon and Rose seemed confident it would be a boy. A grandson!

"Have you heard from Michael yet?" Deborah asked.

Leon shook his head.

"I'm sure he won't come at all," Rose replied, on the verge of tears.

"You're always thinking the worst, Mother," said Deborah in an effort to comfort her.

Michael did not come to the graduation celebration in his honor, not even when the last dancers left the Plaza at three-thirty in the morning. He did not come home that night, even at four o'clock when Rose and Leon each took their medicines and recalled the most pleasant incidents at the party. He did not come home and did not call in a message to the answering service to say what had happened.

"He's angry," Rose said, sighing.

"Do you know why?" Leon asked without expecting a reply. "Does anybody know why he should be angry?"

"He could of at least said something." She turned off the lights. They pretended to sleep.

Because Michael was youngest, Leon and Rose designated a birthdate for him after the girls; they chose November 7 because it was thirty-one days later. When Rose asked her husband why it had to be thirty-one days, Leon replied that he vaguely recalled the number from childhood being related to the number of days after birth when a father takes possession of a son. When they changed Naomi's birthdate, they chose the first day of Chanukah—the Festival of Light, no longer minding their preference for celebrating the girls' birthdays before Michael's. Michael had cheated them of the pleasure they had anticipated for his twenty-first birthday. When they had proposed the same kind of lavish party they had organized for his sisters at the Tavern-on-the-Green, Michael fumed as if facing his own execution. By the time they proposed a quiet family dinner, he was already out of the house. They proposed no festivity to mark his twenty-second birthday, but placed a check for ten thousand dollars on the desk in his room, where he would be sure to find it upon his return from classes. They refused to be cheated of a graduation party in his honor. In their mind, it would be the last sumptuous family festivity, celebrating special occasions past, present, and future. They hoped desperately that he would not disappoint them.

Chapter 12

DEBORAH

"Abracadabra," he intoned in a shrill falsetto. "What we see is not real, what is real we cannot see!" For a fleeting instant, the coin seemed suspended in air, then vanished.

The dark-eyed girl giggled.

He showed his palms. Empty.

The prestidigitation was repeated several times and the magic formula incanted. Soon even his companion looked away. The rumble of the engine drowned out the whispers and whimpers.

"Dumb cow!" he roared and put a threatening fist under her nose.

She scowled, her lips turned in biting mockery.

"Fag," she whispered. Then raising her voice: "Fag, fag, fag."

"You don't understand," he whined.

"I don't have to understand. Your analyst gets paid to understand. This is the first day in a week you've spoken to me and that's what comes out. I won't put up with it. Get out now or I'll call the police."

Sidney hurled himself on the floor, encircling her ankles with his arms. He kissed the tips of her velvet slippers. "Please, Debbie. Give me time. I'll work out this problem. Please!"

She stepped out of his grasp and moved toward the telephone. "I'll call if you don't get out now."

He rose and straightened his clothes, smoothed the flowing pocket handkerchief. "If that's what you want."

"That's exactly what I want."

"I'll send for my things tomorrow. I'll get a lawyer."

"Fine."

For a few moments he stood transfixed by the open door as if trying to piece together the shards of their three-year married life. Inchoate. A jungle.

"Dumb cow!" He slammed the door.

She went to the nursery. Their two-year-old daughter was asleep. The old Negro lady who had cared for her and Naomi from the day they set foot in America lay on a sofa, knitting by a soft light that did not shine on the side of the room where the child slept.

"You heard?"

"Yes. It didn't wake the baby, though."

"You understood?"

"Some men are like that, I guess. They can't help themselves. Except for the bad talk, he's not a bad man, I don't think, Miss Kane."

"You think I should tell my mother and father and sister?"

"You had better sleep on it. When your head's straightened out in the morning you know better what to do."

"What are you knitting?"

"Something for the baby."

"Good night, Cassie."

"G'night, Miss Kane."

Deborah filled a tub with steaming water. She pressed a button on the bathroom wall. Through speakers in the bedroom and bathroom poured the pseudo-Oriental music of *Turandot,* her favorite opera.

Naked, she stood in front of the full-length rose-tinted mirror. You're so goddamn fat, she silently told her reflection. Tomorrow you start peeling it away. As she sprinkled lavender bath crystals into the tub she purred the first aria, her voice loud enough to cover Birgit Nilsson's voice, soft enough to hear the music.

Dumb cow! She felt like vomiting.

"Dumb cow!" Sandy Green snapped at her. The seventh-grade teacher had placed Deborah next to Sandy Green and Naomi was seated beside Harriet Stark. The teacher vainly tried to get the two class newcomers to say a few words calculated, in her mind, to establish rapport with the other children in the class. A classroom filled with strange faces two days after their arrival and without knowing more than a dozen words of English: it was overwhelming. Naomi's smile and composure gave a sense of familiarity, of strength. Deborah sat and looked blankly, absorbing sounds and colors. She pretended not to notice the teacher. The children tittered.

"Do you know that you are in the United States of America?" said the teacher to Deborah, hoping for a simple yes. Deborah stared uncomprehendingly ahead, or so it seemed.

"Dumb cow!" Sandy Green snapped. Loud deliberate laughter, forced high-pitched giggles. She knew the derision was aimed at her, her dark strange appearance, the heaviness of body, the clumsiness of movements, the apparent lethargy. She turned to Naomi. A glance inquired. Naomi shrugged. The teacher reprimanded Sandy Green, but the other children including Sidney Kane took up the chant, Sidney clapping his hands in glee.

Unable to curb the periodic outbursts of mockery, the teacher tried to tutor Deborah and Naomi in English. Naomi shone. Deborah disappointed. Indifferent and apathetic in spite of countless drills, her speech remained a hodgepodge of several European languages in which English gradually dominated. By the end of the first year at Hartley Deborah's teeth were straightened, her front teeth completely capped, and her smile a radiant testimonial to dental technology. The piano teacher reported to Leon and Rose that it would be well to consider another instrument, since Deborah responded poorly to piano lessons. The dance teacher reported that while Deborah had a marked sense of rhythm, her clumsiness prevented any basic mastery of ballet or modern dance and was certainly a cause for embarrassment, since the other children in the studio could not be restrained from taunting her about her size. Deborah had three sessions a week with the school psychologist. The reports reflected no insights Leon and Rose had not already perceived themselves: normal intelligence, sluggishness but no motor anomalies, difficulty in breaking through her emotional defenses.

The only cheerful, affirmative reports about Deborah came from Madame Hermione Reichmann, a voice teacher. In conversations with Leon and Rose, she praised Deborah's natural ability. The director of Hartley was right in recommending voice lessons—considering Deborah's ease with foreign languages, her innate sense of rhythm, her genuine response of pleasure to sounds and moods and the fact that there was no competition, no other children around to taunt or hinder Deborah from mastering a skill in which she could feel justly proud.

"Of a doubt, not a scintilla," proclaimed Madame Reichmann. "Inside of her, a huge talent she has. And when her peak she reaches, there will be a great flowering talent of a rich soul living in her like an infant waiting to be born."

Rose was warmed by the flowing, extravagant praise. Even if the smallest part of it was true, it helped efface the many negative reports.

Leon asked, "How long does it take for such a talent to reach maturity?"

"By the time she's thirty if she's a contralto." Madame Reichmann's voice was melodious and assured. "If she's a soprano, it could be. . . ." She hesitated. "Ah, it could be when she has her first love affair."

"What's the connection?" Leon asked.

"Is she a soprano or a contralto?" his wife asked.

Deborah entered the sitting room and curtseyed awkwardly before Madame Reichmann.

"Debbie, darling," her mother said, "your teacher says you have a beautiful voice and are going to be a very talented singer."

"I'm nothing but a dumb cow," she replied and sullenly left the room.

"Beautiful," the voice teacher chirped. "How beautiful and high-spirited. I see her singing Leonora!"

"We have had to learn to be patient," Rose said, sighing.

"What's the connection between her voice and love-making?" Leon insisted.

"Talented girls who have their first big love affair by the time they are twenty, twenty-two, all become sopranos."

"Why?"

"That has been my experience in the opera. It may with the glands have something to do."

There was no love affair at age twenty or at twenty-two. Other than school parties during high-school Deborah had no dates. At graduation she sang the "Star Spangled Banner" and, toward the end of the program, a selection of songs from the popular Broadway musical *Carrousel*. There was much animated applause, but none of the boys who may have been entranced by her moments of glory on the stage asked her for a date, not even her distant cousin Sidney Kane, the son of a third cousin of Rose's. There had been no boys at the summer camps to which she had been sent and while she listened raptly to the girlish tales of romantic conquests, including the sexual precocity of her sister, she did not participate in the late-at-night storytelling. It was the same for the two dreary years she spent at Clarendon, a fashionable junior college for girls. At parties, polite partners were scheduled for the dark-eyed, dark-skinned wallflower. There were dances and the feeling of being held close in a young man's arms, his knee pressing between the folds of her crinoline gowns, but no dates, no romance, no love affair. At the Clarendon graduation ceremony she sang the "Star Spangled Banner." Afterward, Madame Reichmann told Leon and Rose that Deborah now had all the qualities to be trained as a contralto, urging that she undertake voice study on a full-time basis.

A week after graduation she began her study as an opera singer with Austin Flemming, who, after his last performance of *Boris Gudonov*, retired from opera and opened a studio. Some of the men and women who studied with him were already performing supporting roles at La Scala, the San Francisco Opera Company, the Metropolitan, and Chicago. Four hours a day in his studio, another three hours a day in her home. At night, Deborah settled down in front of the television set with Cassie.

"You better wrap your pretty throat around with woolen scarves, Miss Debbie, when you go out tomorrow. It gone to rain real bad."

"The weather report on the TV is for fair and cold. They didn't say rain."

"Well, the circus is coming to this town. And when animals are in a town, it's got to rain real hard."

Many nights were spent listening to Cassie's superstitious warnings of dire events and to Cassie Deborah confided her loneliness. Many nights were spent playing dominoes and checkers or knitting with heavy needles.

"Cassie, I want to fall in love and get married."

"People have no say over that. God does things like that all by himself. When I was a little nothing of a girl I worked from dark in the morning till dark in the night in the fields and my aunt and uncle were just no good drinking all the time. They beat me with greenbriar switches so hard I must have bled every day. Once they throwed a stone so hard in my stomach for lying in the fields dreaming the day away, that it must of mixed something up inside of my being a woman so that I could never have a baby. I kept dreaming away that a man would come along and say 'Cassie, I want to love you so much and be your husband,' and so I waited and waited till God did what he has in his mind to do, and a man came along and saw the whipping I was getting from my aunt and uncle and he just knocked my uncle over like he was nothing but an old fencepost all broke down and told my aunt to go home and soak her crazy head in cold water. He took me away with him and we were married the next day. I was thirteen years old about and we was married thirty-four years to the day when God took him back like the day he gave him to me. And that's the way it'll be with you."

On their twenty-sixth birthday dinner they were dressed in formal attire. Cassie brought in two Rumplemayer birthday cakes aglow with candles. Deborah pretended to wish for something and blew out the twenty-six flames with a short burst of breath like the dying gasp of the Bohème. Her twenty-sixth year had just died, she thought as she cut portions of the cake and handed them around the table: first to Rose who would only touch her little finger dipped in the icing to her lips since sugar was forbidden, then to Leon, who would ask for a second helping, then to Cassie, who would eat her portion in the kitchen, a dainty slice to Naomi, who would leave half the portion since she was still trying to control her shape after the birth of little Harriet six months earlier, and a final slice to Naomi's husband, Robert, who would annoy them the rest of the evening by insisting that male ballet dancers were all fags and women dancers all nymphomaniacs.

There was still an hour before the ballet and Leon asked her to accompany him to the library. Rose, Naomi, and Robert went into the living room to listen to Robert's undeniable proof regarding the sexuality of ballet dancers.

Leon fingered the leather-bound volumes, collections of works on Lincoln, the collected writings of Tolstoy, Dickens. Begin by beginning, he told himself. Deborah stood beside the windows overlooking Eighty-Second Street; from the opposing windows, the bluish phosphorescence of a television set and the silhouettes of children watching. She stood so as not to crease the gown in the deep leather library chairs.

"Debbie," Leon began. "You know that your Mother and I love you."

Rekindling the old theme, she thought. But it was usually together with Rose. His talking to her alone meant that there would be a variation on the theme.

In his deep gravelly voice he summarized his feelings of affection for her, Naomi, and Michael.

She noted that his hair had become quite thin, the gray had changed to a soft white, the once firm lines of the jaw had a look of pudginess where the skin sagged. There was no paunch; he was still lean and vigorous: golf, massages, and steam baths maintained a leanness that led people to believe that his genetic equipment had indeed passed in toto to Michael.

"In life, Deborah, you can't always make things happen. You have to allow things to happen. You may not like him, but. . . ."

She realized she had not been listening. "Who?" she asked.

"I was talking about Sidney. Your cousin, Sidney."

"What about Sidney?"

"Your Mother and I think it would be a good idea if you and Sidney got married."

She burst into a rich contralto laughter. Pure theater. Sustained, controlled. The next gesture would have been to grasp a papier-mâché dagger and hold it triumphantly above her head, a laughter of abandon slowly transforming itself to glacial mockery. In the other hand, the head of the deceiver, treacherous victim to her regal wrath. She feigned a gasp for breath.

"In time"—Leon's tone was even, practiced, reserved as in a straightforward business transaction— "In time you will love each other. Not at first. In time you will have a family, common interests, and your life will be full and happy. Your mother and I would like this for you. For your own happiness. Sidney is a good boy. He doesn't have a profession, but I can take him in and between Robert and myself, he'll learn. He has a good head. He will be a devoted father and husband. In time you will love each other. We know many families. . . ."

Before they went to the ballet she acquiesced as she had with every other facet of her life since she was adopted. Throughout the performance she thought of Sidney as her lover, her husband, the father of her unborn children, and could not help control short fits of giggling. Sidney Kane! Mrs. Sidney Kane, she imagined herself writing, on letters and sales slips at Bonwit Teller. He did not correspond to an ideal lover or husband for the simple reason that she had never been able to shape one in her imagination. Why not Sidney?

The only awkward event at the spectacular marriage at the Plaza occurred when Deborah took it upon herself to introduce Fay Buttonwood to Leon and Rose. Rose chatted lightly with the girl, was polite, friendly, then quickly busied herself with the excited guests. Her daughter was to be married. Leon walked away without extending his hand to her. "Father," Michael called, but Leon did not turn back. No one tried further to change his mind. The rabbi's speech alluded to the devotion of the family to Jewishness, to Sidney's curiosity and pursuit of truth, to Deborah's voice that would someday become celebrated throughout the world and the numerous and generous benefactions of Leon and Ruth Howard.

At five o'clock, Deborah and Sidney Kane left the ballroom and changed into ordinary clothes, Deborah threw the bridal bouquet. In accordance with custom all the unmarried young women gathered in a circle to be the lucky one. Michael had asked Fay Buttonwood not to join the circle. She agreed. When Harriet Stark shrieked with joy at catching the flowers, both Deborah and Sidney hugged her and left the festivities. It was the day before Christmas when they arrived in the bridal suite at the Fontainebleu Hotel in Miami Beach.

Sidney performed his marital duties thoughtfully—in silence and without passion. Deborah enjoyed the novel physical sensations. They were pleasurable; the touching, the tranquillity. After the second week at the Fontainebleu, his silence caused her to purchase a record player and many records of her favorite arias. Before entering their bed, she pressed a button to release the first of a stack of recordings, turned the volume on low, and drifted away into a world of sound and color and mood as they went to sleep without embracing, without conversation.

Refusing to swim, Deborah wore a flowing raspberry-colored terrycloth robe and reclined in a beach lounge watching Sidney swim either in the gentle water of the ocean or in the blue-tiled pool. During the long sunny days she nursed a continuous daydream that someday she might look like the slender, shapely, scantily dressed women for whom the sun seemed only a justification for baring much of themselves to the critical eyes of other women and the ogles of men. A gentle sense of fondness for Sidney developed when she noticed that he never once let his eyes stray to another woman. Almost blatantly, as if to reassure her that his attentions were for her alone, Sidney played ball or swam alongside a lifeguard or other young man. Although they went promptly to their honeymoon suite after a late-evening dinner and dancing, unlike other newlyweds and other couples at the hotel, Sidney did not partake in the cocktail hour with her before dinner.

After the first week in Miami Beach, he regularly left her in mid-afternoon and returned at seven to shower before dinner. She didn't inquire and there was no reason for suspicion. She was content in every way. She imagined that life for most newlyweds was very much the same, even though it did not correspond precisely to the descriptions she had heard from her sister Naomi. What bothered her, perhaps all that bothered her, was that Sidney seemed to be unable to initiate a conversation on any subject and when she happily and gushingly told him her thoughts and feelings about opera, clothes, where they would live when they returned from the honeymoon, even morsels of conversation about the possibility of children, Sidney seemed distracted or increasingly indifferent. She did not mention that Sidney was to begin working with Leon on their return, for fear that it might embarrass him. She did not allow herself to ask Sidney to speak words of endearment to her for the same reason. An arranged marriage, she thought, like an adoption has special rules. One can't be like others. Her passivity increased as the days went by and she gained weight. Two nights before the end of the month-long honeymoon Sidney entered the bed where she had been waiting for him, perfumed, arms outstretched in anticipation, the second act of *Traviata* playing softly in the background, a vase filled with a cascade of purple-and-white hyacinths, the moonlight shining in from above the ocean, the silk sheets into which a delicate lilac scent had been sprayed, and, for the first time, broke his taciturnity. He cleared his throat with a cough. "Debbie, I can't. For some reason, I just can't."

She pulled her arms back, crossing them across her bosom. "Are you sick?"

"No."

"Is it something you ate?"

"No."

"Did I do something to displease you?"

"No."

"You find me repulsive because I'm heavy!"

"Nothing like that. I just can't."

Sidney fell quickly asleep as if exhausted.

Her large, dark eyes remained open until the automatic record player made its last mechanical click, until her senses became indifferent to the scent of the hyacinths and to her own perfume, until the moon set, until the darkness obscured the man's body beside her, until she could recall with certainty the overheard conversations of the girls at Clarendon and at summer camp that a man's performance was occasionally erratic, that there was a reason, and that a woman had to discover the reason. On the last night of the honeymoon Sidney simply said good night and offered no excuses for his apparent exhaustion. And for the next month they simply shared the bed without conversation, without intimacy. By that time, tests showed her to be pregnant. Sidney was relieved rather than overjoyed when she told him the news.

When Sidney began his job with Leon, Deborah saw less and less of him. She continued her lessons with Austin Flemming until the seventh month and limited practice at her home to only an hour a day. Sidney, when not out of town on business, returned past midnight and had taken to sleeping apart from her in the guest room so as not to disturb her rest, and he was gone before she was awake in the morning.

From Naomi who had been told *in secret* by Robert, Deborah learned that matters between Sidney and Leon were going from bad to worse. Sidney didn't keep appointments, was offensive to clients, and contemptuous of employees.

Finally, Leon provided Sidney with a fund of one hundred thousand dollars to allow him to start his own business in whatever field he wanted. When the transaction was completed Sidney bought a chain of men's hairdressing parlors. He allowed Leon's accountants to inspect his books balance sheets and, as long as he operated in the black, relations were diplomatically correct.

When the baby was four months old, Deborah resumed full study with her voice coach. Sidney was rarely at home and as infrequently performed conjugal duties. At breakfast one morning Deborah announced that she was again pregnant and expressed a desire that this time it would be a boy. Sidney showed no emotion. He interrupted his customary silence.

"Deb, I've been seeing an analyst for more than a year now. Three, sometimes four times a week. I'm going to tell you something because my analyst says that it'll be far worse for both of us if I don't."

"I don't want to hear it," she exclaimed in a burst of protest.

"I've got to tell you. Listen, will you?"

"No." She wrenched herself from his grasp and started toward the baby's room.

"Debbie, I'm a very sick human being. Please, I beg you." His cheeks trembled. The first sign of emotion in almost two years. His face was pale, his hands shook. Tears streamed from his eyes.

She wanted to take him in her arms and console him.

"I've probably hurt you by never telling you that I love you. I couldn't. I didn't love you when we married and I'm not sure whether I do now."

"You're crazy. What are you saying? Why?"

"Please hear me out. I can't love you, not just yet because I can't really love any *woman* just yet."

"What have you concocted? You hardly speak to me for almost two years and now this garbage. Have I been hateful to you all this time? Is that what you're trying to say? Is that why you had to go to an analyst? It was an arranged marriage, pure and simple. No promises. I would not have been hurt if you wanted to back out. But now, what is this ugliness?"

"I've learned, you've got to understand, that I'm ambivalent in my emotions, in my makeup. In time I'll work it out. I want it to go one way, but I'm pulled in the other. Damn! I want it to go in the way of loving you and really being your husband, but I need time. To be by myself to know whether I really long for one direction or the other, or whether I'm really deceiving myself. I want time and understanding. I'm asking you to be patient and understanding and to help me. Help me, Deborah."

"Ambivalent!" The tone was pure mockery. "Ambivalent—what? I don't understand. I hear the words and don't understand. All it means is hatefulness and ugliness. I don't want to hear any more. I have a baby asleep, a beautiful baby and there is another one growing inside of me. That's all I know. Please, not another word."

"Ambivalent means that I have strong attachments to you and. . . ."

"And what?"

"And men."

Her jaw hung agape. She pressed her fists against her temples. "I don't understand. I don't understand!" she shouted.

"Debbie, it means that sometimes I feel sexually attracted to you. Other times I feel attracted to men. That's what it means. I'm sick. I'm sick. I need your understanding and help. It'll change, I know. With your help, it'll change."

She ran her hands down the sides of her body, grasping the outside of her thighs, wanting to pinch, to tear.

"You've made love to men?" A hoarse whisper.

"No," he answered. "But the *desire* is there."

"Get out!"

"I need your help!"

They shouted insults and threats at each other. He opened the door. "Dumb cow!" It was the voice of a malicious child.

The Oriental music of *Turandot* seemed to come alive and dance in the hot vapors that streamed from the tub. For a moment there was a sharp pain in her womb, so strong, so agonizing that she wanted to scream for Cassie. It subsided. The bath water was pinkish, but she thought it was the bath crystals. In the afternoon she went to the hospital, certain that she would miscarry.

Chapter 13

NAOMI

Naomi read aloud to her two daughters. They wore flannel nightgowns printed with Mother Goose characters. They hugged soft dolls as she read to them. In a few minutes they would be asleep. Robert entered the room and kissed his children tenderly.

"Mommy will finish reading tomorrow," he said, tucking in their blankets. He gestured with his head, indicating that he wanted Naomi to leave the room. The children did not protest. She covered the two girls with kisses and left the room with Robert.

"Why the big rush?" she asked. She wore a satin maternity gown, flowing, but cut deftly along the sides to show her well-shaped legs. She was well built but not beautiful. High cheekbones, a strong chin, intense, bright-blue eyes. An interesting, striking, intelligent face but not a beauty by any standard. Nose too strong, brow too wide, fingers too long and too expressive; qualities which, in smaller quantities, would give at least the appearance of prettiness. Her presence tended to overwhelm. Wherever she appeared with Robert, she looked less formidable, even fragile; Robert was over six feet; he had preserved the look of the college athlete.

"Who in hell is Ida Kaminets?"

The tip of her tongue traced the outline of her lips with a light coat of moisture.

"Would you like a drink before dinner?" She cocked her head as if indifferent to his question.

"Yes. I would very much like a powerful drink before dinner. Before that, I want to know who the hell is Ida Kaminets."

She mixed drinks, humming.

"Why do you want to know?"

"I have a right to know."

"Your right to know depends on my right not to let you know. You're the lawyer, so you should know that. If I knew why you wanted to know, I might recognize your right. You're not a tyrant. Or are you?"

His tone softened.

"This afternoon, Judge Lieberg asked me to come up to his office. He had spent the morning with your parents drawing up their wills. Obviously, I couldn't be privy to the terms of the wills, but the judge told me that they had considered anyone who might possibly, conceivably, be in a position to contest the will. Only one name came up and Lieberg suggested that I ask you. The name was Ida Kaminets. Now, do I have a right to know?"

"The past," she said, shrugging, "it just doesn't want to stay asleep."

"Yes or no?" he asked impatiently.

"When we met for the first time handing out campaign leaflets for Kennedy, I tried very hard to avoid you. I was silly with excitement by just being near such a wonderful hunk of a man. I wanted you to approach me, I would have done anything to lure you away somewhere for myself, even for a quickie affair. I stood you off though because I was afraid. Everything in my life until then was planned to the last detail. Mother and Father wanted it that way and I didn't protest. The boys I went out with, even serious dates, were boys from families that had my parents' approval. There could be no accidents, nothing by chance. I didn't protest, because it suited me fine. With strangers there would always be the risk of their questions. Falling in love crazily, wonderfully the way we did, would mean having to face someone prying open something that I decided to shut forever. I was prepared to marry one of the boys from school whom I liked, really liked but didn't love because I was on familiar ground. I pushed you off that first day when you asked me to dinner and the second and the third times and I cried myself out each time because I wanted so much to be able to fall in love with you. And we did fall in love finally. And when you made me a woman and offered to make me honest by making me your wife, I was happy; I just can't tell you how much. Part of it was the fact that until then there were no questions. Oh, you did ask, of course, but I avoided them in every possible cute way. Let's dance, Robert, tell me about the preparations for your bar exam, how did the moot trial go, let's go to the park and make a snowman. Remember? Yes, you do, I know. It was only just before our wedding that the questions came fast and furious. Bang, bang, bang as if I were in the witness chair. I said that I was going to tell you as much as I chose to. The camps, the war, the fact that we were adopted. Then I asked you to promise me one thing and if you agreed I would never ask for another promise. Do you remember the promise?"

"Yes." Robert blushed. "I remember."

"Only questions about the future, never again about the past—neither to me, to Debbie, nor to Michael and under no circumstances to my parents nor to anyone about us three children. You made that promise!"

"Yes."

"Then you don't have the right you say you have."

"No. But the circumstances. . . ." He squirmed.

"We can't live according to 'circumstances.' We can only live according to what we want. And I don't want to relive something that's dead, buried, and forgotten."

"Forgive me, Naomi. I'm sorry."

She grasped his face between her long fingers and kissed him. "You're forgiven, darling. Now that you are well behaved again, I will tell you about Ida Kaminets because there's something very beautiful about her that I want now to share with you. If I didn't, Ida would stick in your throat and in your imagination she would be distasteful. And she's not. She's everything that's the opposite of evil and ugliness. Until now she was a private joy among Debbie, Michael, and myself. A childhood secret that couldn't be shared. I'll tell you, but on one condition."

"Okay."

"The condition is that you will never again bring up our past or ask about it. To me. To Debbie and Michael. To no one."

"Does that include our children?"

She hesitated and her eyes glanced about the large room as if her reply were written on one of the walls.

"If the promise applies to the children, the ones in there," he said, jerking a thumb in the direction of the children's bedroom. Then he pointed to her swollen belly. "And that little fellow in there. If the promise applies to them, I definitely won't give you such a promise. They have a right, an absolute right, to ask and to expect the truth from us. I'll lie till I'm blue in the face when I have to protect a client, but I'm not going to lie to our children either by telling them things or by failing to tell them what they want to know. You can't expect that of me."

"All right." Naomi replied, exhaling deeply as if relieved. "The promise excludes the children. If they ever ask, *you* will answer them."

Robert smiled, waiting to hear about Ida Kaminets.

"Then," Naomi began, "when everything was upside down in the world, it was illegal to adopt children from DP camps. There were agreements between governments, between armies. Everyone had agreements except the children in the camps. We were only political ammunition. No one could be adopted until we had been resettled as one large group. And that particular detail was going to be the object of an agreement between governments for years. There was enough red tape to strangle on. Ida Kaminets was able to break through it. Judge Lieberg was able to take care of the legality and the papers and everything that you lawyers like to play with. We see Ida from time to time. Sometimes a year will go by without seeing her. She's away somewhere. We have no idea. Sometimes we'll see her every week for a few months. I never really know."

"She arranged the adoption then?"

"Yes."

"Was she paid?"

"I don't know. Michael, Debbie, and I give her money whenever we meet with her. Is it important?"

"Depends on the purpose."

"To help her continue to do for children today what she did for us then. As long as she's alive I'll continue to do that."

"Much?" he asked meekly.

"That's not your concern, is it, Bob?"

"I'm sorry I asked. But I see clearly now what Judge Lieberg was concerned about. There is the slight possibility of a contest."

"Does it matter?"

"It did, before. Much less now after what you've told me."

"Did the judge mention to you that I brought Ida Kaminets to my father two or three years ago."

"No," he answered with surprise. "Only that anything about her I should find out from you."

Naomi recounted the meeting.

She did not want to bring Ida Kaminets to Leon's office. The huge desk was forbidding, telephone interruptions were certain; the heavy drapes, signed photograpshs by famous political figures, the distances between chairs would be overwhelming for Ida and provide Leon with the opportunity of making a decision too quickly, abruptly, and harshly. When she sought the advice of Deborah and Michael they said that Benjie's wasn't a good place, either: Leon would be resentful of the shabbiness of the place and it would reflect adversely on Ida and what she was doing. An arranged "accidental" meeting would arouse his suspicions that he was being trapped. The meeting couldn't take place in Deborah's home because of his dislike for Sidney and, without mentioning it, they didn't suggest a meeting at wherever Michael might be staying out of respect for Michael's wish not to make any kind of appointment with anybody. Discussion of where to arrange a meeting between their father and Ida Kaminets went on over a period of weeks. It was finally decided that the best place to meet would be in the visitors' lounge of

Beth David Hospital after a trustee meeting. Psychologically, Leon would be in a philanthropic frame of mind and receptive to both Ida Kaminets and the idea she was urged to propose. Except for some simple articles of furniture, there would be nothing to intimidate either. It was a place that stirred Leon's most generous sentiments. By the time they had agreed that it was the best place to meet, Ida informed them that on the very afternoon of the day set for the meeting, she was sailing for Le Havre. As a result, they met at the pier.

"I want you to talk to a friend who's leaving for Europe today," Naomi told him. They crossed the long, chilly dock. It was the last transatlantic crossing of the autumn. There were only a small number of passengers, no parties, nor the traditional colors and excitement of departure. Naomi looked for Ida in the tourist-class passenger lounge. She sat in a quiet corner reading as they approached.

"Father," she said, "do you remember Ida Kaminets?"

He paused, adjusted his horned-rimmed glasses, and studied the puffy face of the aging woman.

"You are the one. . . ."

"Yes," she replied. "I'm the one, Mr. Howard. Please make yourself comfortable." She gestured to the purser, who promptly brought a platter of stale sandwiches and three small bottles of ginger ale.

Leon turned quizzically to Naomi.

"I may never return," Ida Kaminets said. "Children's enemies would like to see me dead or in prison. For them children are chattels to be used in a vicious game of politics. So many thousand children for so many inches of territory. So many thousands of children for so many million barrels of oil. It used to be just Jewish children that could be bartered away. Now there are many more. There are twenty-two million refugees in our miserable world, Mr. Howard. Twenty-two million. Black, white, yellow, red. More than half are children. Most will never know where they were born or who their parents were. Many will never know parents at all, only camps and packages of canned food from America. Their lives are being bargained away for rivers, lakes, and ports. Their health is being bargained away for machine guns and tanks, their childhood sold for control of the arbitrary lines of frontiers, drawn across deserts and mountains. Most of the organizations supposedly concerned with these refugee children are in reality military mercenaries in the pay of governments that seek advantage through the tragic problems created by masses of refugees. They are not interested in the swollen bellies of children dying from hunger. They are not interested in typhus and the other diseases running rampant in the refugee camps. They're interested in keeping refugees where they are to help gain some political advantage for those who pay them. Twenty-two million of them, Mr. Howard. Ten percent of them die each year from hunger and disease, if not at the bloody hands of those organizations who are playing dirty political games with their lives. Yes, they're all guilty, the Red Cross, the Save the Children Federation, and all the others working for the *kill the children* governments. You are a generous man, Mr. Howard. A rich man. At one time you helped Jewish children. You are still very generous when Jews are concerned. But there are millions. . . ."

Leon did not allow her to continue. He got up and with a gesture grasped Naomi by the elbow, a sign that they were about to leave.

Nervously shaking his head, his face flushed, he said: "I have my charities, I have my commitments. I am grateful for what you did in helping us adopt our children. You agreed then that we would never see each other again. I am sorry that you broke that promise. Naomi, you will probably want to say a few words to Miss Kaminets. I'll wait for you on the pier. Don't rush. I'll wait."

"The ginger ale is flat," Ida said. "Not cold enough."

"I'm sorry Ida." Naomi threw herself onto the woman's bosom and wept.

"Your father is a very generous man. His compassion is very deep. He is very honest about his feelings. He is helping where he can. The others, they'll be helped, those who survive."

Naomi removed her gold wrist watch, a brooch, gold earrings, and pressed them into Ida Kaminets's hands. Ida looked at the meticulously designed, exquisite jewelry. A thin smile appeared at the corners of her mouth.

"One for the earrings, ten for the brooch, four for the lovely watch. Fifteen children. Fifteen children will live another year because of this beautiful, inanimate junk. You had better go, Naomi. I'm going to scold the captain for allowing ginger ale to be served without bubbles. Good-bye."

"Do you think we should stop?" she asked Robert.

"Yes."

"Are you asking me to stop?"

"Would it do any good if I asked?"

She smiled.

"About me, Robert, what do you think?"

"In what way?"

"I mean that I have no background. My life begins from the time of the DP camp. I've no ancestry, no pedigree, no coat of arms. Does it bother you?"

"No. I love you, Naomi. I love you for who you are and not because of or in spite of your ancestry."

She kissed him with fervor. "It doesn't bother you one single bit?"

"To be very honest, I'm curious as hell. I mean you could have been Russian or Greek or Spanish. Anything. Your real parents could have been anything. I mean I'm curious, but that's all."

"I could have been not Jewish, too. Probably I was not Jewish. Does that bother you?"

"Off the bat, no. It doesn't seem to make a bean of difference. I never thought about it in terms of myself, either. Like one day you're told that you're Jewish and you go to synagogue and have a bar mitzvah and make contributions and that's about it. I'm proud of being Jewish. I would never have thought of marrying a girl who wasn't. But I don't quite know what it really, genuinely, means to be Jewish. If anybody were to ask me what it means to be Jewish, I guess I wouldn't be able to answer. Do you feel Jewish, honey?"

"Yes, I do."

"How?"

"I'll tell you someday."

The maid appeared at the door of the living room. She carried a white telephone and a long extension cord. "It's your mother, ma'am. She seems upset."

As she spoke, the color drained from her face.

"What is it?" Robert asked.

"It's Debbie," she answered, handing back the phone to the maid. "She just separated from Sidney and is in the hospital. It may be a miscarriage. My god"—she shuddered—"poor Debbie."

Chapter 14

THE PASSING OF AN AGE

"That's where the ducks used to paddle around, remember, Leon?" She pointed to the ice-skating pond. It was a huge circle illuminated by high-intensity fluorescent lights. It was close to midnight; a dozen skaters moved gracefully to the music piped in over hidden loudspeakers. Blades hissed against the artificial ice.

"They were geese, not ducks."

"I know the difference between geese and ducks," Rose protested. "And I say they were ducks. Ducks and geese are different. Ada Lynn used to help Abe's grandmother pluck feathers to make pillows."

The rugged pastureland had been contoured, manicured into formal gardens, golf courses, tennis courts, riding paths, formal gardens. Wooden frame farm buildings that had first housed Mountainview Hotel in its early years had been torn down; there wasn't a trace that remained. A gleaming fifteen-story marble cylinder stood in its place. A feat of engineering skill had hollowed out the granite beneath the surface; for three storys down there were boutiques, cocktail lounges, playrooms, saunas, and restricted rooms reserved for gambling.

"Ducks, geese, what's the difference?" Leon shrugged.

Fifty seasons at Mountainview were coming to an end. A full moon washed the snow-covered lawns with a white radiance. When Rose's cousin first converted the played-out farm into a small hotel, only forty people could be accommodated; now, on a holiday weekend, there were usually more than three thousand guests. The season did not run from the Memorial Day through the Labor Day weekends: Mountainview was filled almost to capacity the year round. It had become, as Leon had anticipated, a confined city, a city of luxury, a city palace for working people with its own airport; celebrities vied intensely for the chance to make an appearance at Mountainview; conventions were booked at least two years in advance and the health center, sandwiched in between the first and third below-surface levels, was spacious and equipped as well as any modern infirmary.

"It's so strange," Rose said. "With the full moon and the snow, it's like daytime at night."

"Daytime at night," Leon teased. "What kind of sense does that make? Moon. Snow. Fields. Remember, Rose, when we were kids we used to shut the window tight at night when the moon was out?"

"To keep out the angel of death."

"No," he protested. "You were supposed to get TB or something. The day after the full moon we had to wear little bags of camphor tied around our neck to go to school. We stank up the whole classroom. No, it was for TB or something like that."

"I'm glad children don't have to grow up any more with foolish superstitions. You know what Ericka said to me on the telephone the other day?"

"What?"

"She said: 'Grandma, there's no God. Because I just looked up his name in the telephone book and it wasn't there.' "

"She said that?" he asked proudly.

"She did."

"Smart kid."

"At five, I think that's smart." Her eyes caught the graceful bounds of a young deer leaping across the snow-covered meadow. It vanished in the woods. A dark wisp of smoke trailed across the full moon.

"It's chilly," she said. "Shall we go back to the party or go to bed?"

"We'll go back to the party and say good night to everyone first," Leon replied.

Two in the morning. The orchestra was still playing. As the two of them appeared in the ballroom doorway, the orchestra leader asked the musicians to strike up the anniversary waltz. It had been that way since the dinner-dance celebration had begun. A silken banner hung across the full width of the ballroom: HAPPY FIFTIETH ANNIVERSARY, ROSE AND LEON. Only three layers of the twelve-tiered cake remained on the huge silver platter.

Abraham Breen had brought together a special selection of Mountainview's three hundred most steadfast guests, many of whom had actually, at one time or another, spent holidays at Mountainview at the same time as Leon and Rose. It was his offering of gratitude; the anniversary date was still a few weeks off.

Those who had not yet congratulated the couple approached them and in the flush of excitement caused by an excess of champagne and dancing kissed both Leon and Rose and shook their hands, reluctant to let go.

"How beautiful everybody looks!" exclaimed Abraham Breen. "My father would have said that even the czar couldn't have such a fine party. All my friends. All working people enjoying the fruits of the earth. Caviar and champagne! Imagine. So many of the guests were greenhorns without a pot to piss in. Now there's peace of mind. Contentment. Happiness. It's so wonderful to see everyone dancing and having a good time."

"It's a wonderful party, Abe," Rose said. "Thank you from the bottom of my heart. We're going to call it good night now."

Handshakes. Expressions of gratitude. Bear-hug embraces. They eased their way across the ballroom smiling at each face, touching hands, waving, blowing kisses. The music would continue until the last dancers quit the floor. Sunrise, perhaps.

"My feet are so swollen," Rose sighed, removing the gold-embroidered satin slippers.

In honor of their fiftieth wedding anniversary, Abraham Breen had arranged for their suite of rooms to be redecorated. Everything reflected the latest style in luxury furnish-

137

ings, except for the "knicknacks" as Rose called them—the infinite number of small objects she had accumulated at Mountainview over the past half century. Leon was in his pajamas and robe. Rose sat, in her nightgown, beside a ruffled vanity table, brushing her white hair with short, quick strokes of a hairbrush. Leon brought a small mirrored tray on which he had arranged a glass of water and several plastic phials containing an assortment of different-colored pills.

"You still have some toothpaste on your cheek." She extended her fingers to brush off the white paste. Her hand remained, lingered on his cheeks for a moment. The skin sagged, there were bags under the eyes, liver spots on the temples and forehead, a crown of white hair on the back of his head.

"Here's the pink one for diabetes," he said. "The white one for high-blood pressure, one for you and one for me. The blue one for the swelling and the red one ... I forgot—what's the red one for?"

"In case we can't get to sleep. It's for sleeping."

"Here's the whole secret of being senior citizens." He smiled as he shook the phial with red capsules.

"Down the hatch."

Rose stood up from the vanity-table seat about to step toward the bed. A sudden look of bewilderment crossed her face. She tried to recall the name of the waltz played by the orchestra. Or was it the name of a grandchild of one of the guests? Or the face of her cousin, Abraham?

"No ... I mean ... what was it, Leon?"

He had already removed his robe and was sliding between the sheets. He noticed her puzzled expression. Before he could rise from the bed, before a question could form on his lips, Rose sank slowly to the floor. Slowly, slowly ... a balloon slowly deflating, slowly and soundlessly. She had not fainted: her eyes were open like those of a child looking at new surroundings. She sat propped against a leg of the vanity table, her own legs awkwardly turned—one folded, the other outstretched—the swollen ankles blue and throbbing. An unblinking rag doll.

"Rosie! What is it." His voice trembled.

"I don't understand," she whispered.

Breathing with difficulty, he dragged her to the bed, raised her, with whatever strength remained in his arms, the short distance to the sheets. Carefully, he propped the pillows beneath her head. The white hair seemed strangely disarrayed. His hand rested on a forehead that was cold and clammy to the touch.

"What hurts?"

"Nothing."

"Do you feel all right?"

"No."

"So what's wrong?" He raised his voice, a hint of anger.

"Don't shout, Leon."

"What's the matter?"

"I just don't feel good, that's all."

"I'll call the doctor. There's always a doctor on duty."

"No, I don't want a doctor. I'll be all right."

The left side of her face sagged; her left arm hung limp and lifeless. Her eyes were huge frightened circles.

On the other side of the bed he raised the telephone. The switchboard operator answered. He told her to send the house doctor to their room. Replacing the telephone, he slid across the bed and caressed his wife's forehead. They waited.

The doctor entered quietly with a pass key. Leon looked up at the face of a man his own age—gray, stooped, a face lined with the bitter truths and ravages of a long life. There was something about him that seemed familiar, someone from another age, perhaps.

"Everyone calls me Dr. Mac," he said with a gruff smile. He sat at the edge of the bed and grasped one of Rose's frail wrists between his fingers. He grunted. The stethoscope disc was placed against a thin blue line on the woman's neck. He kneaded the flesh of the limp left arm. No reaction. He pulled the sheet exposing her legs. The left leg was limp, useless, the swelling of the ankle like a useless, weighty collar.

Dr. Mowiss squinted at the hypodermic syringe. He plunged it into a vein. They waited.

"Haven't we known each other, once?" Leon said.

Dr. Mowiss turned his face up to Leon. No recognition.

Not the slightest trace. He shook his head, clicking his false teeth that were fit badly behind sunken cheeks.

Her eyes closed. The breathing steadied.

Leon sensed relief. With a gesture, he inquired.

"She's dying."

"Oh, my god." Leon stood motionless, his hands spread against the pajama legs. "Shouldn't we get her to a hospital?"

"It wouldn't help. It's a massive cerebral hemorrhage. I gave her a shot to make it easier for her to breathe, but it's a matter of maybe a few hours. That's all." From the bottom of his black bag, Dr. Mowiss took out a bottle of French cognac. He fetched glasses from the bathroom. They drank.

"Will she wake up?" Leon asked.

"One chance in a million."

"She won't wake up?"

"Forget it."

"Just like that. Dying is just like that."

"Easy come, easy go."

"We were married fifty years, almost."

"The party was for you?"

"Yes."

"I didn't go. I don't like parties any more."

They drank.

Leon searched the man's face. There was something that recalled the past. Something familiar about how the doctor sat, even though the bent shoulders deformed the lines of the body.

"Were you ever attached to Beth David Hospital in Brooklyn?"

"No," answered Dr. Mowiss indifferently, sipping the cognac. "Never."

"Funny, you look like someone I once knew."

"Old people like us all look alike."

"I guess so. What time is it?"

"Almost three."

"It's late. You've seen many people die, I suppose."

Dr. Mowiss shrugged.

"Is it easy? Like Rose? For Rose it looks easy. Is it easy for everyone?"

"Yes," he grunted.

Leon put on the robe he had draped over an armchair and pulled the chair beside the bed. With one hand he grasped Rose's, the other he kept free to handle the glass of cognac that Dr. Mowiss refilled from time to time.

There were long stretches when neither spoke. When it seemed he was dozing off, Dr. Mowiss wrapped an elastic band on Rose's arm and squeezed a rubber bulb to get a reading of her blood pressure. Leon looked on the act, hoping that the doctor would say something to the effect that her condition was improving. He said nothing. Senseless, ritual gestures: pulse, stethoscope, a finger against the carotid artery, kneading of the lifeless muscles. Soon, they both fell asleep, slumped in chairs by Rose's side. When the first russet and yellow streaks of dawn entered the room, they woke and realized she was already dead.

More than five hundred people attended Rose's funeral: Leon's business associates, friends, recipients of generous benefactions for over forty years, distant cousins. The rabbi who officiated at the funeral service depicted her as an ideal wife, mother, and philanthropist for the needy, the sick, the lonely. He spoke glowingly of her devotion for her three children. Of her children, only Naomi and her son-in-law, Robert, were present. Neither Deborah nor Michael could be located. Her grandchildren were there, fidgeting and whimpering, tended by their nurses.

Leon died peacefully in his sleep exactly thirty days later. There were many more mourners at his funeral than at Rose's; the obituary in *The New York Times* was a column long, describing him as a multimillionaire. Many of the mourners were total strangers, eager for a glimpse at the remains of a rich man. Naomi and Robert came to Leon's funeral, but Deborah and Michael again could not be reached. At the cemetery, a grave was ready for Leon beside Rose's, around which fresh shoots of spring grass had sprouted. At the entrance to the plot was a small, marble footstone hard to notice in the crowd: "Ada Lynn Howard/1927-1939/Beloved Daughter/In Eternal Memory."

Louis Lieberg, lifelong friend of Leon and Rose, delivered a graveside eulogy. Several times, his voice cracked and tears came to his eyes; several times he seemed to forget what he was saying and repeated himself. The theme of the eulogy was Leon's love. He concluded: "In an age that is moving fast away from the ideals of respect, honor, and love, we have lost a beloved friend who has helped make that age a glorious one, one not to look back upon, but up to. Beloved friend, good-bye."

The rabbi recited a final benediction and the crowds walked away from the fresh gravesite to the waiting limousines at the exit gate. One man remained. It was Dr. Malcolm Mowiss. He stood at the child's footstone, a smirk on his lips, muttering that at last luck was to give him the definitive chance for choosing life.

Chapter 15

ARTICLE XI

Judge Lieberg's voice crackled as he read; he had to stop from time to time to wipe away the tears and blow his nose.

"In accordance with the instructions of your mother and father, as their lifelong attorney," he said, "and as their lifelong and closest friend, I have filed their wills for probate." He brushed his hand over his mane of soft, flowing white hair and went on.

"Michael, Robert, and myself are named executors of both estates. Your mother's will is relatively short and inasmuch as she disposed of the bulk of her estate before her death, may she rest in peace, there are only minor points that you can examine at your leisure. Leon's will runs to ninety pages and it would be pointless to go through it word by word. That too, if you wish, you can do at your leisure. As far as your mother's will is concerned, the only new element is jewelry and household effects. These she divides equally between Deborah and Naomi. You two girls can work out whatever you want in that regard."

They nodded.

"Be guided by your personal preferences, for I think that is the spirit Rose intended. Leon's will, in spite of its length and copious legal boilerplate, is rather simple." He changed his eyeglasses and held the sheaf of papers close to his face.

"Two million dollars are to go for the hospitals and medical-research centers he has been supporting for close to fifty years. A million outright, the balance from estate income paid out over the next ten years. He has stipulated that after taxes and so forth the estate is to remain intact, including all income from the estate, until you each reach the age of thirty-two. At that time you are to receive the nonbusiness portion of the estate in equal shares. Provision is made for token shares to his grandchildren. If the estate were to be shared today, each of you would receive something in the vicinity of from four to four and a half million dollars. The auditors estimate that each share will, by the time you each reach thirty-two, appreciate to something close to six million. I'm going to be seventy-six pretty soon but I hope, with continued good health, to live to see you enjoy the good fortune Leon intended." His pink skin glowed and he went on quickly to mention the generous amount that Leon had left him personally; he read slowly, in measured and precise tones, the warm expressions of friendship that Leon had written into the will.

"Now we come to article eleven." He cleared his throat and fidgeted with his eyeglasses. "There's a bit of a problem here. It's so unlike Leon and I must confess to you that when the will was drawn I fought like the devil with Leon about it, but without result. He made it clear that this was his intention. He wouldn't yield so much as an inch. The essence of article eleven is that if you Michael, Deborah, or Naomi, should marry a non-Jewish person between now and the time you reach your thirty-second birthdays, you are to receive no part of the income and no share of the estate. If that should happen, the shares are divided differently. Moreover, I should add that Leon's corporate holdings, developed and undeveloped properties are, according to other provisions of the will, amounting to something like twelve million and will come under the control of the foundation he set up with your mother. For the next twenty years the income from these real properties will be paid to a prescribed list of charities; about a third of the income will go for this. The remaining income is to be invested by the foundation officers. At the end of twenty years, the corporation is to be dissolved and the proceeds from the sale are to be divided in equal shares among you and your children. However, article eleven also governs here. If any of you or any of your children marry a non-Jewish person during the next twenty years, neither you nor your children are to receive any portion of the proceeds from the dissolution of the corporation and its holdings."

Michael and Deborah exchanged glances, glances of hurt and anger. Naomi and Robert sat quietly, looking at the pink face of Judge Lieberg.

"You may resent the conditions of article eleven. They probably come as quite a surprise. Leon was not a fanatic about anything. In matters pertaining to Judaism he had a very open, very liberal point of view. Did he ever express his intentions along these lines to you?"

Michael and Deborah shook their heads. Naomi said, "No."

"Just a few more words," Judge Lieberg said restlessly. "Because of the sheer bulk of the estate and the fact that there are over forty institutions that are beneficiaries of the estate, it'll probably take about a year until everything is finalized. It should be smooth sailing—that is, of course, if no one enters a contesting claim. That's most unlikely." He folded his glasses and blinked his eyes sleepily. They understood it was time for his noon-hour nap.

They walked down two flights of stairs to Naomi and Robert's apartment. It was on the same floor where Deborah lived with her daughter and where Sidney had lived until the separation. Another flight below was the apartment where Rose and Leon had lived.

Robert prepared cocktails. They were all silent, waiting to see who would speak first.

Naomi said, "So we don't know who we *were*. But we know who we *are*. That's the only thing that's important. Father wanted to make sure, to remind us always who we are. The wealth and comfort he and Mother gave us is nothing compared to their taking us into their home and into their hearts. We are part of them."

Irritated, Michael blurted, "He could have done that without all this Jewish-identity crap. What *is* being Jewish? Is being born into a Jewish family Jewish? Does article eleven make us Jewish?" He slammed a fist into an open palm. "He's put the same damned ring through my nose dead as he did when he was alive. A goddamn golden ring."

Deborah stared at the bar, her large dark eyes on the verge of tears following the deft movements of her brother-in-law. Mechanically she reached to the other side of the couch and found Naomi's hand. The firm grasp was reassuring.

Naomi spoke in a self-confident, cheerful voice. "Robert and I are raising our children as Jews. We're not fanatics. Yes, we go to temple with the children and we look forward to it. The children go to Sunday school for religious instruction and we're proud of it. The children can't wait to go, they love it. We don't observe any kosher things because that's silly. We observe all the important holidays because they're beautiful and give a rich, wonderful feeling to us and the children. I'm Jewish because that's how people react to me. They treat me as Jewish. Everything from the sneaky comments and the jokes to the charitable appeals. What difference does it make who my real parents were or what they believed? Being Jewish isn't in the blood. I used to stay up a lot at night crying and wondering where I came from, who my parents were. There were fantasies, dreams. But from what I hear from other mothers, all children, even when they know who their parents are, have the same fantasies and dreams. At some time everyone wishes they weren't what they are. That's all finished. Someday, Robert and I will tell our children about my past, when they're old enough to understand, when they're old enough so that it won't make any difference. I am Jewish. I feel Jewish."

"He had no right to play god," Michael snapped.

"Get off it, Mike," Robert retorted as he placed a highball glass in Michael's hand. "It was *his* dough."

"I wouldn't have cared if he didn't leave me a red cent," Michael said. "That wouldn't have bothered me. But he's holding out a carrot from the grave. Be a good boy, do what I tell you to, and when you grow up there'll be a big bundle waiting. Strings attached! With him, everything had to have a string attached."

Robert grinned. "Not everyone's going through the hippy, flower-child thing like you. What you call strings, others call responsibility. I have a hunch that Father was afraid you might go up to the top of the Empire State Building with a million bucks and throw it to the wind, bringing peace and contentment to the wage slaves and five-and-dime girls."

Michael glared at him.

"I think you had better stop that, Robert," Naomi cautioned. "Michael's entitled to his point of view."

Deborah struggled with her words. "Too much. They gave too much. Everything we wanted, whenever we wanted. It was too much. Jewish? I don't know." There had been discussions with Austin Flemming, her voice coach, about marriage, but not terribly serious ones. She was eager but unsure.

"You know," Naomi said in a tone of surprise, "I think the will is a way of keeping us together as a family. Mother and Father want us to stay close together, to preserve the family in the way they would have liked had we been their own, their very own children, their very own flesh and blood. We have been close. We'll be even closer now."

Michael said, "More strings. Don't you see? He wouldn't take any chances. Stick together, not because you love each other and want to stay together, but because it will pay off in the long run—in dollars and cents."

Deborah lost interest in the conversation. She looked about the room with a vague expression. At night it would be good to be away from all this talk and in Austin's arms. In the darkness she didn't have to think about his age.

"Michael," Robert said firmly, "you're looking at the matter in the worst light. It's a cynical point of view. You could also say that because of your closeness to one another Leon felt that the capital would be secure, not dissipated. When families are at each other's throats their dough is swept away."

"I agree," Naomi said.

"You could turn almost anything around to make him look good," Michael protested. "The fact of the matter is that none of us, including you, Robert, really knew him. And he certainly never really cared about knowing us."

Deborah got up and started toward the door. "I'm going. I've some things to do."

"I've got to go too," Michael said. They kissed, shook hands, and agreed to see one another soon.

Leon's phantom voice and hand were deciding events and for two of his three children caused unplanned grief.

Michael handed his sister into a cab and walked west across Central Park. Yellow forsythia blossoms were everywhere; branches of crabapple and barren cherry were about to burst with white and pink flowers. The grass was pale green, tender, abundant. School-age children played ball, sprinters ran foot races, dogs tugged at their leashes.

I couldn't care less, Michael thought, hearing an echo of Judge Lieberg's voice telling about the immense fortune waiting for him. Even the hundred thousand dollars a year from Rose's trust fund gave small satisfaction. Little of it ever got to be used; his satisfactions declined as the spending increased, but not the other way around.

The abortive two-month career as a race-car driver in Acapulco only produced a fractured right forearm and a cast for three months. The much-vaunted excitement, colors, crowds, danger, and terrific speeds offered little pleasure then and less in retrospect.

Some kites hung lazily overhead, strings dangling limply. Like parachute jumping in Biarritz. Just wet, that's all. He had sold the twin-engine Piper, bought a diving rig, a thirty-six-foot cabin cruiser and motored to Sardinia. Zero! Absolutely zero! He recalled the guttural shouts of *grazie, grazie* when he dumped the gear on the sand, swam back to the cruiser, and went god knows where next.

"Twenty-four," he said aloud, catching the attention of some children passing by on roller skates. I tried it all. Zero! What the hell would I do with the millions even if I had them today? He sat on a bench and fixed in his mind the revery that occurred more and more frequently since Rose and Leon died. He savored the sweetness of it and

148

was angry at himself after it was over. His real mother and father, tall good-looking people, hard-working, living somewhere in a miserable hovel in Europe, struggling with decency for a better life, taking part in secret political meetings aimed at overthrowing oppressive governments and liberating mankind—they were farmers in Greece, rag pickers in Budapest, factory workers in Bucharest. He strolled, kicking a top a child had lost along the path. Horses cantered on the bridal path. Outside of Albany he had bought a stable and five thoroughbreds, complete with trainers and handlers. The races were dull. The whole thing lasted five months.

Twenty-four and all I can do is spend money, waste money, and make much more than I can possibly use even if I lived to be a hundred.

It was a block and a half to the brownstone on Ninety-Third Street. That was a pleasure, he thought, the only real satisfaction that the money had ever given. The top floor had been converted into a floor-length studio for Fay. The second and third floors had been rebuilt to make a duplex: one vast living room led up the winding steps to a floor of bedrooms and baths. On the street level, the rear garden portion had been made into a large kitchen; the front part was not used, but Michael had plans to use it eventually as a garage.

He let himself in through the ground floor. Flowers in many vases. Art books filled every space in the floor-to-ceiling bookcase; they all belonged to Fay.

"Fay?" he called at the head of the stairwell.

"Be right down," she answered.

She danced down the marble steps in her bare feet. She wore a mini-skirt in lemon-colored silk, her long legs still very tan from the weeks spent in Puerto Rico. There were smudges of paint on her arms and cheeks. They kissed perfunctorily.

"Everything all right. It went all right, I mean?"

"How would you like to convert to Judaism?"

She picked up a velvet pillow from the couch in front of the marble fireplace and threw it at him playfully.

"Well, I've often thought about becoming a Buddhist."

"I'm serious," Michael said.

"Or a Hindu, or a Christian Scientist."

"Come on, Fay. I'm not kidding."

"Or a scientologist or something far-out and spooky like spiritualism."

"Would you convert to Judaism?" he insisted.

"Why should I convert to anything? I'm very happy the way I am. I only believe in you and me. That's it. The *summum bonum,* or something like that I learned in Latin classes. Isn't that enough to believe in—you and me? When I pray, I pray for you and me together. I pray to life, to beautiful things, to eyes and legs and lungs and things like that. I pray that you will always love me the way you love me now." She threw him into the long couch, entwining her long arms about his shoulders. "Do you love me now? Will you always love me?"

"Uh-huh."

"That's the extent of your adoration? Vile creature!" She began pummeling him with her small fists.

"I'm suffocating."

She stopped. "I don't want to convert to anything. Believing in anything, I mean, really having faith and crap like that is completely hypocritical. I don't have to rationalize it scientifically or anything logical, but I had a dose of catechism when I was a girl that was enough to sicken me along with the hypocrisy of my mother and father and aunts and uncles. I mean the whole scene was mass distortion and perversion. I have nothing against Jesus, but for crying out tears—the horrible things that people do to each other in his name. It never bothered me that the priests and nuns goosed us every chance they got. I can understand that and that's not what turned me off on religion. It boils down to all the religious people trying to carve everyone else's heart out in the name of some god. I don't want any part of it."

"If I marry you now, in your pagan state, you little sexpot shiksa of mine, I forfeit all of my rights under the will."

She frowned. "Does money mean that much to you?"

"That's not the point."

"That is the point!"

"I don't know."

"You don't know what?"

"I don't know if money means that much to me or not."

"Well, you're saying that it comes down to my converting or you not getting an inheritance. Isn't that the point."

"Okay it is."

"Well, what do you want?"

"I'm not sure."

She jumped from the couch and glared at Michael. "Screw you!" she shouted.

"Come on, honey. We can work it out. Let's talk seriously."

"No. Not really. If you don't know what you want, then there's nothing to talk about, is there?"

"What's the big deal about converting?"

"It's plain hypocrisy. As long as we've lived together and there's been no talk about getting married, everything has been a dream, beautiful! Now, the first time you open your mouth about getting married there's a hitch. Convert? I was perfectly happy not being married. Marriage is bourgeois, outmoded stuff. I never asked you to marry me. You know, Michael, for someone who hates things with strings attached, you have strings up your sleeves. If you're proposing marriage, forget it. I'm not interested."

"Suppose we had a baby while we were living together and then we wanted to get married, would you consider?"

"I don't want to talk about getting married. I don't want to talk about having children. Right now, thanks to you I feel crawly and creepy all over because all I mean to you is some kind of collateral. You know what, Mr. Rich Man? All of a sudden I dislike you intensely."

She was out of the house even before Michael realized that she had slammed the front door. He ran out to the street. At the corner he saw only her long tanned legs slip into a taxi. He wanted to shout, to call her back. The cab sped away.

On entering the living room he lit a marijuana cigarette. Deep, hissing inhalation. Bitter smoke. How many had they smoked together? A million? This would be the first time in ages he had one by himself. She'll go to a movie, have a Chinese dinner, and be back here around eleven. She may even call from outside and ask me to join her. He looked at himself in the oval mirror over the fireplace.

Straight brown hair pulled back without a part. Straight nose, thin face, narrow shoulders, incurably underweight. A small dark mole on the right cheek just under the ear. "You're a Jew, Michael. You're a Jew. Jew, Jew, Jew, Jew, Jew, Jew. Leon Howard said you are a Jew and don't ever forget it."

Through the amber haze of the smoke the reflection could have been a seven-year-old child, dark and brooding, dressed in rags, standing on an endless line of thousands of children each holding a metal cup, waiting for soldiers to ladle out a portion of steaming broth containing small pieces of bread and cabbage. The child's face streamed with tears. The revery was disturbed by a pounding on the front door. He smiled, convinced that Fay had already returned.

It was his brother-in-law Robert, his face bloated with rage. Michael feigned calm. He asked Robert to come in as he lighted another marijuana cigarette.

"Just after you left," Robert said, trying to catch both his breath and his composure, "I got word from Lieberg that two people have filed claims against the estate."

"Is that unusual?" Michael asked indifferently.

"You better believe it," he said, gesturing wildly. "One of them is a woman claiming a million dollars. The other is a doctor claiming a hundred and fifty thousand dollars."

Michael laughed. "So what?"

"The woman said she left a million dollars with Leon years ago, for safekeeping, and now she wants it back."

"Maybe she did."

"Balls, she did! There's no likelihood of that. The other claim is from a Dr. Malcolm Mowiss. He claims that he gave medical treatment to Leon and Ruth."

Michael forced the smoke out between his teeth.

"Lieberg says he has no recollection of the doctor, except for the one contact the doctor had with Ruth the night she died at the Mountainview Hotel."

"Is that so?" He reclined on the couch with an air of total imperturbability.

"Do you know the doctor?"

"What's his name?" he asked, pretending not to recall.

"Mowiss. Malcolm Mowiss."

"Maybe. I'm not sure." His face was lighted with a large smile.

"Michael." Robert was fully composed now. He had assumed the professionally calm manner of the lawyer. "These are, no doubt, nuisance claims. People read the obituary columns and see a chance for a long shot. But sometimes, contests take years to resolve unless the claims can be quickly negotiated. If we knew them it would be a different matter. Naomi doesn't. She called Deborah and she doesn't know either one. How about you, Mike?"

"What's the woman's name?"

"Safire. Yvonne Safire."

"Nope. I'm sure I never heard of her."

"And Dr. Mowiss?"

"I'll have to think about it. I'll call you tomorrow. I'm kind of upset about things right now. I'll think about it and will call you tomorrow."

"Mike," Robert began, "I know you don't like to be tied down. I know you like to be free to move about: here today, somewhere else tomorrow. If you're not around to help us fight these claims, the whole thing can drag on for years. The losses to the estate can be very substantial."

"I'll be around," Michael answered noncommittally. "I'm kind of tired of knocking around, you know. I'll be around. I'm thinking of getting married."

With a shocked uplifting of his eyebrows, Robert said, "Fay Buttonwood?"

"Maybe. . . ."

"But you know what that would do?"

"Yes, yes, yes. I know. But then again maybe I should give my kingdom for the woman I love."

"Would Fay convert?"

"No. Maybe we'll just get married. Just like that." He snapped his fingers. "Screw the money."

"You're not serious, Mike?"

"No, I'm not. I'm just sick to my stomach as if I've eaten a bellyful of uncooked potato peelings. Have you ever eaten raw potatoes?"

"No."

"Disgusting." He got up from the couch, picked up the brass fireplace poker, raised it over his head, and brought it crashing into the mirror. "Dammit! Dammit!"

The blow sounded a crackling, screeching whine. Two lines appeared, forming a jagged V.

Terrified now that Michael might turn on him, Robert stepped back and instinctively held his hands to his face.

Michael threw the poker to the floor.

"I wouldn't hurt you, Robert. I've got nothing against you. I even like you. I just didn't like the fucking mirror. It makes me sick."

"Mike," Robert said helplessly, wanting to help, sensing his brother-in-law's anguish.

"Just go, will you? I feel like puking."

He waited until three in the morning for Fay to return; when she didn't he made a telephone call to her father in Pittsburgh, awakening him, frightening him. No, they hadn't heard from Fay. He called Fay's sister in Poughkeepsie. She and her husband both got on the phone; their voices sounded like they had been drinking. Music and party noises boomed in the background. They hadn't heard from Fay in months. He made random calls to hospitals, giving them a description of Fay, insisting that they check the emergency room. There were no accident cases or emergencies that fit her description. It was futile. A soft, pale, rose-colored light, the light of morning, suffused the room. He swallowed two red capsules and threw himself on the rug in front of the fireplace, hot angry tears streaming from his eyes.

Chapter 16

THE SONG OF DEBORAH

The nocturnal visits with her voice coach had assumed a mechanical regularity and become steadily joyless and monotonous. The intimacies were hasty and matter-of-fact. The arias she had learned so easily, the pronunciation she had mastered with great difficulty, the music she had once considered as something belonging to her, ceased to give even a shred of pleasure. The first few weeks with Austin in bed were exciting and explosive, the way matters should have been when she was nineteen or twenty, but weren't. Then Austin cut out the preliminaries: a token bottle of wine in place of the original delicacies and champagne, a record in place of the first hour—she singing, he at the piano. She entered, they ignored the wine, and undressed on the way to Austin's bedroom. Deborah's departure was as robotlike as her arrival.

Austin's first advances to her coincided with her loss of forty pounds and the consequent change of clothing to a much smaller size and a fashion suitable to a woman of twenty-nine who was rich and almost slender. It all took place quickly and she was stunned that she could awaken feelings in another human being. His rooms were filled with photographs of leading operatic performers, opera-poster announcements in a multitude of languages, and large, glossy pictures of himself with celebrated impressarios of America and Europe. Although he was close to sixty, gray, endowed with a large paunch and promptly snored after their perfunctory love-making, he was the only man who had ever, other than Sidney, expressed tender feelings toward her or attempted to persuade her to undress and go to bed. At first she had a fantasy that this man who had sung the role of Boris Gudonov at the Paris Opera in 1930 was the same virile-looking, handsome figure that looked out from the vestibule poster with intensely powerful and brooding eyes. After a while there were no fantasies either about sex or about singing. She was the first to leave the bed; as she slipped on her dress and arranged her bracelets, Austin, putting on a velvet dressing gown, said, "Deborah, my dear, you have changed. Perhaps 'changed' is too limiting a word for what I mean to say. You are transformed. I hardly recognize the person I came to know a year ago. Physically, of course, there is a great difference. But in the transformation, something was lost."

"My voice!" She laughed and searched for one of her shoes.

"Yes, the spirit is gone from it."

"I never really wanted to sing, you know. I studied voice. I think I loved it because I had nothing else I loved. It came easily, I think, because it was a language without being a real language. Just beautiful sounds that didn't have to mean anything. I'm tired of singing. I think that I'm beginning to be interested in other things. You wouldn't appreciate it, Austin, never having married or fathered children, but I get a lot of pleasure these days from my daughter. I never realized it before. I had a child and cared for her, but she was like everything else, including my voice—indifferent. Something is changed. I agree with you. And I think you have something else that's on your mind. Speak out. I assure you I won't be offended."

"Between us, my dear. . . ."

"It's over," she said calmly. She daubed her cheeks with powder. "It's been over for some time. I guess even sex can become a habit like so many things."

His tone grew businesslike: "You should give yourself to assisting young performers to achieve greatness. That would be so valuable, my dear. It would only be a trifle for a wealthy, very wealthy woman who, like yourself, is sympatico to the performing arts."

Her jacket was on and a pocketbook slung over a shoulder. Her thick, dark lips framed an ironic smile. "If I set up a scholarship fund for young singers—"

"Fantastic," Austin interrupted. "Divine!"

"For young sopranos, let us say—"

"Darling, you're wonderful." He took her hand and bent to kiss her fingertips. She pulled her hand back.

"It would be very interesting for me to encourage young singers to study voice with you. Suppose I did just that, Austin. Would we continue to see each other? At night? In bed, I mean?"

He clasped his hands on his breast in a gesture of prayer. "Anything you wish."

"I'll let you know," she said, walking toward the front door. They entered the vestibule; it was arranged like a Spanish patio with colored ceramic tiles on the floor, tall, potted palms against the walls on which metallic-looking swords, opera props, were hanging.

The doorbell rang loudly. He tightened the robe cord around his waist and opened the door a crack.

Deborah heard a voice ask if it was the home of Austin Flemming. A familiar voice, but the words pronounced too softly to be sure.

"I am Austin Flemming," she heard him reply.

"Is Deborah here?"

"That's none of your business!" Austin tried to force the door shut.

Deborah looked at the widening crack in the door, her knees trembling and a strange, apprehensive pounding in her heart. Her lips suddenly became dry.

The door was thrown open with such force that Austin almost fell backward. Sidney stood there, his fists raised to chest level, his knuckles white.

"What do you want?" Austin stammered. He couldn't retreat, as he would have wanted, into another room. Deborah blocked the passage.

"I'm her husband."

"Sidney!" she gasped.

Sidney reached out to her, ignoring the voice coach who

stood between them. He took her hand. "Let's get the hell out of here."

"Over my dead body!" Austin shouted, mainly in defense of his wounded pride.

"A pleasure!" Sidney shouted back. His fist shot out, striking Austin on the end of his bulbous nose. Austin reeled, cried out as if mortally wounded, and fell backward against the wall between two potted palms. Then he slid to the tiled floor, knocking over a palm and bringing down on his head a rubber stiletto that bounced across the vestibule.

The throbbing in her heart diminished slightly; she was suffused with a tingling sense of pleasure and well being. They left, and she entered the car without question or protest.

"Deborah, I love you. I'm going to make you understand that. I was sick and couldn't love you or anyone else. I'm not sick any more. You're my wife. I'm proud of that. I love you!"

Sidney drove northward. They continued well past the point in the parkways where there ceased to be road lamps and illumination, only the car's headlights. She sat tensely by his side, her body quivering, feeling an intense excitement that she had never experienced before. Her cheeks were flushed. Finally! she thought. The words that all the girls in school and camp had told her were the most important thing in a woman's life—"I love you." The whispered conversations during history class, the interminable chatter in the camp bunks, the definitive observations in the college lounge about a man's ambitions, a man's jealous rages, tendernesses—the foreign things she had never understood or felt had suddenly come alive and entered her life. She felt hungry in a way she had never known. They passed through an area of high, silhouetted hills and woods. She felt a wild urge to run, to chase and be chased, an urge to reach out of the car window and pull the dark clouds to her face, an urge to possess Sidney, to fuse his body with her own. Without being aware of how or when it happened she realized that she was pressed against his side, her arm through his, feeling the muscular movements as he maneuvered the steering wheel.

She said yes when Sidney asked if she wanted to know how he had spent the past two years.

"You don't have to say yes, Deb. You don't have to say yes to any goddamn thing at all from now on."

A car passed and for a moment she saw the firm angles of his face. The softness of two years ago had gone. He looked strong and handsome.

"I do, Sidney. Really. I would like to know."

"From now on, Deb, we only do what we want. What we really want. That's been my trouble. Yours, too."

"Yes."

"I sold that idiot chain of wig shops. It made a lot of money. I also did very well on the stock market. I got involved in a land-development thing and did fantastically. I even returned all the money your father gave me—every last nickel and with interest. I moved to Chicago and was lucky to get an honest analyst. Not one of those fifty-five-minute hustlers but an honest-to-god man with strong opinions. I'm all straightened out, thanks to him, and even more thanks to you because I never stopped thinking of you and our daughter for a second. You two are the only important things in my life. I never loved anyone before you, Debbie. I think I didn't know. Now, I do. I want us to start over again."

She didn't reply. His words flowed along, touching and personal, the meaning unimportant.

"I bet you haven't heard a word I said."

"Oh, yes, Sidney. Every word."

"Do you love me?"

"Yes."

"Do you want to know where we are going?"

She shrugged.

They drove in silence the rest of the way.

Gravel rattled and crunched as Sidney drove slowly up a winding path between rows of young cedars and dogwood. He snapped off the car's lights.

"Here we are," he said as he opened the door. Sidney groped in the dark, running his hand along the edge of a wooden post; he turned a key. Like a flood of water bursting from gate valves, the ground on which they stood was bathed in an intense bluish light. Beyond the two-story, massive stone house, a light shone from the top of a cedar to the edge of a steep cliff; a balcony jutted from the rear of the house, overhanging the void below.

"It's ours, Deb," he said proudly. "It was finished last week."

Large rooms with high-beamed ceilings and numerous windows opened out into the artificial daylight of the gardens and woods.

"No furniture yet," Sidney explained apologetically. "Except for kitchen equipment and a mattress upstairs, where I slept while they were putting on the finishing touches. I didn't get any furniture because, well, because that's your job. We never had any of our own furniture, anyhow, because your mother and father did all of that for us. Remember?"

As Sidney gestured, pointing out features of the house she suddenly grasped his arms and pressed them to his sides and, pulling his face down to her own, she kissed him passionately. At length their mouths separated.

"You hungry?"

She smiled. "Yes."

Sidney imitated the sound of heraldic trumpets as he pulled the doors of the enormous refrigerator open. There were a few slices of hard, stale bread, three hard-boiled eggs, and a bottle of plain water.

"I forgot."

"Come on," she said, removing the few things. "Let's have a picnic."

They sat on the floor, eating the bread and eggs with ravenous appetites.

"Debbie, I want us to live together again, forever. I love you. Will you?"

"Yes."

"We'll forget the past. The past is nothing. It's finished, dead."

She leaned forward and placed her head against his breast. Tears rolled furiously down her dark cheeks. Words struggled in her throat. A medley of languages and children's songs sought her tongue. Finally, words shaped.

"Sidney, I love you. I love you."

He made a motion to get up. "Come upstairs," he said, beaming. "There's only a mattress."

Deborah jumped up. "So that's your game," she sang, her soprano voice filling the room. She enunciated the words distinctly as if on the stage of an opera house. Her voice rose in frantic, mock anger: "Ha! The seduction of the innocent maid, Deborah. First you have to find me." She ran out of the kitchen. Awkwardly, tripping and knocking over the water bottle, smashing the brittle egg shells, Sidney ran in pursuit.

"De-bo-rah!" he shouted, imitating a villainous, lecherous basso-profundo voice.

A sustained C-above-C note rose in response from one of the many rooms.

She hid behind doors, in closets. Clumsily banging into doorposts Sidney panted, unable to find her, hearing only the taunting, melodious voice ring out, echoing in the empty rooms. At the foot of the staircase a shoe. Halfway up a second shoe. A scarf. The trail was easy to follow. She had left articles of clothing casually tossed here and there, leading to the bedroom which was to be theirs. But she was not in the bedroom. The mattress lay empty in the center of the room, except for a stocking and half slip. The bathroom—empty. Dressing room—empty. He stood in the doorway of the bedroom, puzzled. He heard a lyrical trill from the garden. Tearing his clothes from his body as he raced out of the room and down the stairs, he was completely naked by the time he reached the garden. He saw her, the bluish floodlights catching the dark tresses and slope of her back as she darted in and out of the tall shrubbery. The branches scratched his skin as he tore through the thicket, yielding tiny smears of blood. Finally, he stood for a moment, wondering where to turn next, and she planted herself boldly in front of him. Her face radiated an enticing smile, throbbing animately from the chase. He was surprised to see her ample body far more slender than he had remembered.

"This is where our garden will be?"

"Yes."

"It will be my garden, Sidney, for me to plant and grow beautiful flowers?"

"Yes."

There was silence as they looked at each other's nakedness. Without a word they lay on the soft grass side by side and embraced. The fire in their bodies obliterated the past.

Chapter 17

THE PARTING

He left the door unlocked so that Michael would not have to fumble with a key. There was no arrangement that he come, no agreement. But there never had been a formal, spoken agreement of any kind between them. It was a silent pact, one that went beyond words, beyond even convenants sealed with blood. It was an agreement written into flesh. Redeem their seed through gold. It could be soiled, spat upon, but not abrogated. He expected a scene of repudiation, but the pact carved into flesh would not be tampered with. The customary scene was expected: father spurned by son; but the father is not father, the son not a son. If it took place this very day it would be done once and for all, and finished. It didn't matter—it could be any other day, any other hour. Time no longer mattered. There was only the tidying up to do, destroying the shards of days long gone. Bitterness and sweetness indistinguishable in the compost heap of the past. Photographs were faded patches on discolored, cracking walls.

Mowiss had finally sold the apartment. The price would permit him to live comfortably for a year without having to scrounge for patients. After the messy, noisy scene Michael wouldn't be dropping in any more, wouldn't be leaving small bundles of hundred-dollar bills on the kitchen table, wouldn't be making out checks to the airlines to carry him to Miami or Tucson, wouldn't be accompanying him any more to men's shops on Madison Avenue for custom-tailored suits which were sold the day they were delivered. But these were only the outward signs of obligation; they could easily be dispensed with, hardly missed; the pact went beyond all trivia.

The thirty days given him to vacate the premises were rapidly coming to an end. His plan was predicated on a handsome settlement offer, within a few months at most. "What if," he asked himself aloud many times each day, "they take forever to make a settlement offer?" He would stop, chomp on his false teeth for a moment and answer, aloud, "We'll see."

Cardboard boxes were to have been filled by now, but nothing was packed in the boxes. Alongside of each lay heaps of shredded papers and worn clothing that the building porters would have to carry out when he gave the word. Jars, bottles, capsules, and metal tubes were scattered about, dust-coated reminders of pharmaceutical products that had gone out of fashion a half century ago. Dross! Who needs it, anyway? For two days he had taken a room: a single, windowless room in a flea-bag hotel on Broadway in the Seventies—a foul-smelling warehouse of destroyed egos. Pimps, prostitutes, junkies, fugitives from the courts, drunks. Two days of tasteless food in the acrid smoke of a hamburger shop where he spent the day betting on numbers, the races, basketball games—all small bets, all lost investments. How different from the time he could walk into the Peabody, Kidder, Harrington and Wilson brokerage house and have the agents kiss his feet. He was tempted to sell prescriptions to the junkies, but didn't for any trouble with the police would certainly place a settlement in jeopardy. Two days of rust-tasting water were enough. There was plenty of time to find a more suitable place.

Blurred, carbon copies of insurance-claim reports crinkled as he walked over them time and again, dumping files on the floor. Bank statements, brokerage-house statements, check stubs and canceled checks, real-estate advertisements. Trash: the filthy droppings of the ravenous predatory animals that had devoured a fortune. A deposit on life, a mortgage on death. Short handwritten memos of hasty transactions, partnership agreements, were crumbled, then tossed onto the heaps. There was a folder with a presidential seal on it. Honorable discharge from the United States Army Medical Corps with several presidential citations. He sat on the floor, propped against the wall, and opened the file. July 15, 1947. He had remained in service for almost two full years after the end of the war. Photographs in the folder: his arms entwined in those of a strikingly beautiful blonde woman, his officer's coat almost to his ankles, the woman in a knee-length coat, high-heeled shoes with silver bows at the tips, a heavy layer of lipstick painted on her wide mouth. Who in hell was *she?* A woman. A blonde. There were so many. His mustache was full, trimly tapered to meet the up-turned corners of his perpetually ironic smile. He touched his upper lip. Bare. When did he stop wearing a mustache? Mustache? He tore the file in two, then in two again, letting the pieces fall haphazardly. A large envelope: snapshots—hospitals wards, soldiers at the front lines, hills dotted with vineyards, olive groves, prisoners of war, a long column of them marching with their hands atop their heads, nurses, those pretty women with smiles and shapely figures, women from liberated countries, from occupied countries, civilian personnel of the armed forces, women in army uniforms: bedmates, companions for a fleeting night of sweetness. He smiled. With enough time I could dig a grave with my pecker. He crushed them with his hands. Another folder. Military medical reports. A large photograph of an interminable line of soldiers naked from the waist down, their trousers bunched against their boots. He laughed. VD inspection. A million bare peckers. The sun's energy harnessed in a small wrinkled bag: an atomic reaction, an eerie explosive light never before seen by man, shut up tight in a microscopic frantic, squiggling droplet of scum blindly driving, seeking out, penetrating its target. A million bare peckers, a hanging out of privacy. When the settlement check arrived he would travel to Italy, drink the waters, take mud baths, drink good brandy for a change, and get it up for the biggest and perhaps last lay of his lifetime. He sneered and tore the picture. So many are dead. Dead peckers, Ugh!

In a fury he pulled drawers from the filing cabinets and scattered heaped armfuls of papers about the room. He paused, remembering something, rubbing his fingertips ... a photograph. An article. He ran to the mound of papers beside one of the boxes. Hundreds of medical journals, faded but never read, some in the original brown wrappers in which they had been mailed. No, not a scientific paper. What was the occasion? Chaos. Thinking. Remembering was chaos. There were long blank spaces, blackness, at the junctures he could make the right turn. Occasion? Shit! He remembered the diagnosis that had been made in the Bellevue charity ward, the same that he had concluded: arteriosclerosis centered around the nerve bunches on the left side of the brain. Redeem. Redeem me with gold. Photograph. Report. No. A speech. My speech. A sustained warm flow of luminosity. Connections. Goddamn good connections. Not just awareness but awareness of awareness, that's the whole trick, my boy. Shit on senility. You'll make it yet in the as yet unemptied desk. The chronological file. Recollection like a sweet kiss from a voluptuary.

It was not a journal article, but rather the typescript of a speech given in 1952 at a meeting in New York City of social-work administrators. There were about thirty of them, all men, sent under a mandate of the United Nations Refugee and Relief Administration to direct the operation of displaced persons camps in western Europe, camps under the jurisdiction of the commanders of the American military zones of occupation. He had met most of them between 1945 and 1947, and for a while after they met once a month over dinner to listen to reminiscences and to compile a record of experiences. The photograph was inside the typewritten leaves of paper. The totality of his medical, scientific writings: a twelve-page speech. In the photograph he stood on the front steps of a long military barracks building flanked on either side by seventy to eighty boys ranging in age from six to thirteen. In front, kneeling, were the smallest, puniest boys. Kneeling in front of him, his hands on the small body, was Mishka. Most looked alike. Pinched cheeks, vague, expressionless eyes, shabby clothing. He allowed the photgraph to slip to the floor. The speech was entitled: "Ritual and Antiritual Surgery: Some Reflections." The substance of it! Strange that it should have been so completely obliterated until this moment. It began by telling about doctors who had been confined to DP camps—political prisoners escaped from one zone to another. Doctor refugees, doctor war criminals, doctors who had been medical officers in the medical units of Axis armies—all fled into the American Zone. There had been discussions with these medical colleagues: ritual and antiritual surgical procedures. Many were successful even when performed under the worst conditions and with the least possible experience in surgery. There were the Jews who during hostilities had skin from the armpit stitched to the soft flesh of the penis to restore the foreskin. The procedure was normally accompanied by excruciating pain lasting for days, since anesthesia or pain-killing drugs were rarely available. There were those who were not Jews—war criminals, murderers, black marketeers, pimps, escaped camp guards, perverts of every station in life whose sole means for escape and survival was circumcision. "As many as fifty thousand," it read. Difficult, painful circumcision on as many as fifty thousand adult males. He did not mention to the meeting of former camp administrators that the doctors, including himself, who had performed ritual and antiritual surgery had grown rich. Jewelry, money, antiques, property deeds that were more valuable than money when the lands were in countries that had been neutral. Nor did he mention that he himself had performed as many as a hundred such life-saving procedures. He did mention that medicine and surgery draw no political lines. It was the same kind of ethics-free decision made many times during internship and the first years of practice. An infant is delivered monstrously misshapen, lacking in limbs, or, through some genetic quirk, possessing too many. A sudden pull, sudden pressure deftly applied, a calculated, infinitesimally brief motion terminated the potential anguish that *it* would certainly bear for itself, its parents, its world. It was the same kind of ethics-free decision he had made numerous times on the front lines in France and Germany when a lethal dosage of morphine could prevent the outraged agony of a boy on learning that his patriotism had cost him half a face or half a body.

He pulled out the wooden drawer with a fierce tug. It fell with a thud, its contents landing on the floor. His first professional paper was atop the pile, a blurred carbon copy. It was dated July 16, 1947, the day following receipt of his discharge certificate and was addressed to the President of the United States. The image sharpened. It was in a Paris hotel room, where he had stayed through the summer, on vacation, before returning to the States. Crocked. The battered portable typewriter? Where? Gone! The paper was filled with double-stroke "i's" and "l's."

Dear Mr. President: You are certainly familiar with the degrading conditions in the DP camps under American jurisdiction. The suffering victims of Nazism, young and old alike, have learned to survive. They will survive. Medical and health conditions are slowly improving to help them face whatever is in store for their survival. There is a never-ending stream of twenty million refugees making demands on our meager resources and entitled to make demands. But I am distressed by the competition going on among rival religious organizations, who want to claim as their own those survivors who do not know their origin. There are two hundred thousand small children scooped up from God knows where in the destroyed cities and villages of Europe. Those who appear to be in good health are being fought over by religious competitors. All reject those who have lost eyes, arms, legs, the mentally defective, the blind and diseased. There have been raids by these church groups and mass kidnappings of children. To stop the bitter strugglings, some camp administrators have agreed to a plan whereby for a period of one hour the Protestants can pick a certain number of children; the next hour is reserved for the Catholics, then the Jews. In some camps the time of selection and the number to be chosen is determined by throwing dice. . . .

The letter continued for four pages; pinned onto the last sheet was a note on White House stationery: "Dear Captain Mowiss: President Truman is out of the country and as soon as he returns you may be sure that your letter will receive his prompt attention. We appreciate your thoughtful consideration of a problem to which the President has given high priority." He received no further reply. He crumpled the sheets into a ball and tossed it on the heap of trash.

A narrow paper box containing dull scalpels had spilled on the littered floor. All in the fingertips. The feel of it. The exquisite feel of slicing into flesh. Bleeding flesh. Expiration.

"Ah, Mishka, Mishka," he sighed. "My downpayment on survival."

Mowiss looked up from the heaps of shredded paper and mounds of trash. He heard something at the door.

Michael stood there, a scowl pulled tightly across his lips. His eyes looked angry.

Mowiss's voice was hoarse, tremulous.

"Mishka, my lad, you've finally come."

"Crap!" he snapped. "I don't know what it is you're up to, but what you're doing is hateful and wrong. I want you to know that I love you as if you were my own father. What you're doing is a horrible, contemptible insult to the memory of the wonderful man and woman who adopted me. They loved me as their own son. I didn't come here to discuss anything with you or to look for explanations. I wanted to see you one last time. To say good-bye. You're cruel and you're filled with a weird kind of spite. I don't want to see you ever again. I'll never stop loving you."

"You're my ransom, old chum. My golden shekels. My seed. My pact with life." He spoke to the blankness of the door. "I can't help it, old pal of mine. I just can't help myself."

Mowiss reached into his vest pocket and withdrew a tiny plastic envelope containing a round pink tablet. He placed it quickly on his tongue and winced at its bitterness. It would make the difference between accepting a few more blank spots that day, lengthy ones, or having a number of them but of very short duration. Thought wasn't the problem. There was little to think about. The past had expired a long time ago. Only awareness counted. He felt the onset of what was likely to be a short but intense blackening of awareness.

Chapter 18

THE LAST MONTH OF THE YEAR

The clash between Robert and Michael that took place in November was smoothed over. Neither mentioned it. Robert had raised the Mowiss question more emphatically than ever.

The exchange between them occurred on the day that Michael had gone to Mowiss's apartment for his last visit. He was sullen when he entered the office and found Robert waiting by the large window overlooking the East River. Michael wore dark glasses to cover his eyes. He stood at the window beside Robert. They looked out from the thirty-sixth floor of the last Howard building project that Leon had seen occupied in his lifetime. Others were rising, steel girders balancing in the air, helmets of construction workers bobbing like apples. Beyond the river were the dense sprawling factories of Long Island City.

Their shoulders nearly touched, but their thoughts were ages, miles apart.

"Mike," Robert began, "this guy Mowiss is a nut. He's bananas. Judge Lieberg has checked him out. In plain words, he's a crook. He's been in a lunatic asylum and he's the one who dug up that woman who made a claim against the estate. How the hell could you have allowed yourself to get tied up with a bad actor like him?"

Michael pivoted. He tore the dark glasses from his face and hurled them on the oversize leather-topped desk.

"Fuck off!"

"Mike," he said plaintively, "you don't seem to realize the gravity of this. Tying up the estate another few months could have a bad effect on our whole cash-flow situation. We're not in Sidney's boat, you know. He's swimming in cash, but doesn't want to team up. We're going to be in rough shape and there's talk about the bank discount rate going up another point or so. I just can't believe it. Lieberg says you were the one who got that nut Mowiss a job in the hotel where Leon and Rose stayed."

Michael slammed a fist on the desk.

"Get off my fucking back!"

"No, I won't! Ethically and professionally I just can't allow that crook to drag us into court for what is nothing more than a shakedown, nuisance claim. For a couple of thousand we can settle, I'm sure. So he treated Rose once. Just once. You've got to be crazy to ask a hundred thousand dollars to sit and hold hands with a dying woman."

Michael glared. He tried to say something but stammered.

"Here," said Robert, pulling papers from his pocket. "A settlement proposal for the good doctor. Another settlement proposal for his lady friend. We can't go ahead without your signature."

Michael slumped into the high-backed leather chair, staring at the golden pen set that was cradled in an onyx base, a gift to Leon on his seventy-fifth birthday by one of the many charitable organizations that had honored him that day. Michael signed his name on the blue-bound documents that related to the woman's claim. He didn't read the text.

"No settlement for Mowiss," he said.

"Michael, you can't."

"No settlement."

"Keeping this in the courts will eventually cost more than a settlement. Don't you realize how arbitrary and irrational you're behaving?"

"Keep it going in the court. Let it take ten years. I'll use my own money to keep it going, if necessary. I don't care. Deduct the costs eventually from my share of the estate. I couldn't care less. But no settlement."

"Goddammit, Mike!" Robert exploded. "You can risk your share of the estate by shacking up and someday marrying a gentile girl, but I have a right to protect Naomi and our children. I can't accept your rigidity."

Michael's eyes narrowed. He rose slowly from the high-backed chair and as if a current of electricity suddenly coursed into his arms, he grasped his brother-in-law by the neck and shook him violently. His fingers inched around Robert's throat.

"Fuck off—I'm not signing." He released his grip and heaved his weight against Robert, almost knocking him to the floor. He picked up the two legal documents and hurled them at Robert.

Robert unclenched his fists. No. He would not fight. He regained his composure and calmly picked up the papers that had fallen beside his feet.

"Okay. If that's your decision. After all, I'm only the son-in-law; you're the son and heir. There's no primogeniture rule, but I guess you're entitled to a double vote. It's your decision that counts. I'm sorry." He extended a hand of conciliation. Michael ignored the gesture and turned back to the window. He muttered something that sounded like "fine."

In the distance the capped green dome of the Brooklyn Savings Bank stood against the clear winter sky like a giant phallus. Where in hell are you, Fay? he said aloud, pounding a fist against the thick window.

By the day's end, Robert came back into the room with word that Mrs. Safire had signed the release withdrawing her suit against the estate. He added that she had readily accepted the first offer of ten thousand dollars.

"It was that easy?" Michael asked.

"Almost. The stumbling block was her attorney. He's a young guy trying to hustle a living from five-and-dime negligence cases. Judge Lieberg did a job on him with a telephone call. He told him he could recommend him to the county surrogate to handle a juicy estate. A lawyer's dream! A call from the former state attorney general and the promise of an estate commission. It wasn't too big an obstacle. I went to her myself. She's not a bad type at all."

Michael raised an eyebrow.

"Interested?"

"Okay," he replied.

"She lives in a one-room studio in a kind of cruddy residential hotel on upper Broadway. She's sickly and making it on small pensions left to her by two dead husbands. She said that Dr. Mowiss had come to her saying that she was entitled to a very large amount of money because of the baby she had once given up for adoption."

"What?" Michael's face wore an expression of incredulity.

"She said it would be like winning the jackpot in a lottery. The baby? She hardly remembered if she had ever even had one. She vaguely recalled that when she was barely seventeen a woman came to see her and offered to see to it that the baby she carried would be delivered by a good doctor in a good hospital and she would also have a thousand dollars."

"That was Mother?"

"Yes. Sounds just like her, doesn't it? After the baby was delivered she took the money and went to Los Angeles in search of stardom and a husband. That was over forty-five years ago."

"Mother adopted the child, and she died."

"Do you think we ought to tell Naomi and Deb?"

"Why bother them about it!"

"Mrs. Safire is planning to buy a condominium in Florida."

"Good for her."

The telephone rang. It was Judge Lieberg, asking to speak with either one of them.

Michael asked Robert to take the call.

Robert's face flushed; he winced in feigned agony.

"I'll speak to Michael about it," he said, replacing the instrument in its cradle. He sat in a deep chair and began to examine his fingernails.

Michael pretended to be busy with papers on his desk.

"Dr. Mowiss has filed an addendum to his claim. May I tell you?"

"All right," he answered reluctantly.

"The good doctor claims more fees for treating you for a cardiac condition." Robert looked at his brother-in-law

174

for a trace of reaction. There was none. "He claims that he filed his medical report with the Selective Service Board in connection with your draft callup. That you were rejected on the basis of his medical report."

Michael nodded.

"It's true?" His voice rose.

"It's true."

"Do you have a heart condition, Mike?"

"Maybe," he said, shrugging.

"This is a real pisser! It's rare for a doctor to violate ethics and make a patient's diagnosis a matter of public record. Any two-bit magazine reporter can go to the records in the surrogate's office and crank out a bunch of garbage gossip about the rich playboy with a heart condition. Michael, please reconsider."

Michael vigorously shook his head.

Chapter 19

NAOMI'S CONFESSION

"I just can't get over it," Robert said, turning his palms up. "Michael knew this Mowiss nut all along. He insists he didn't know the woman, though."

"But he didn't," Naomi said with certainty.

"Well, one of you must have known her. It's just too incredible that she could appear out of thin air. Who could it have been? Leon? Rose? Debbie? You?"

"Me," she said matter-of-factly.

"You?" Robert winced. "For crying out loud!"

"Not really, I knew *about* her, but only my mother ever actually met her."

"Why didn't you ever mention it to me? When you told me about Ida Kaminets I thought that was it. Is there some kind of weird secret going on?" he asked peevishly.

"Until now I couldn't. I made a promise to Mother."

"Why is it suddenly possible now?"

"Because Deborah learned about it for the first time this afternoon. She said it was all right to tell you. I wouldn't have had she felt differently."

"Well, I must say that the three of you are thicker than blood."

"In ways, Robert, that you may never understand. This is how it is: about Deborah, Michael, and me you know only that Leon and Rose, through Ida Kaminets, adopted us from a children's camp in France after the war. A DP camp. That's about all you know. Because that's all I told you. That's all that anybody told you. After our agreement, you never pushed me to tell you more and I have always appreciated that, Robert. Mrs. Safire made her claim against the estate because she believed that Deborah was her daughter, the same one that she had given to Rose for adoption many years ago. Dr. Mowiss probably put her up to it, even though her daughter would have been about ten years older than Deborah. It didn't matter. Dr. Mowiss was the one, probably, who had arranged the adoption and figured it would be a basis for starting a claim. A picture of Deborah during the last few years would lead anyone to believe that she was the grown-up version of the child that Mother and Father had adopted. They had so much in common—and not by accident. In some ways, they are the same person. Mother and Father went to the camp in 1948 because Ida Kaminets showed them many snapshots of children in the camp, including one of Deborah. She told them she could help make arrangements for adoption. They went to France to adopt a child in the photograph, the one who resembled the adopted child that had died, the daughter of Mrs. Safire. Once in the camp, though, Deborah didn't want to be adopted by them unless they adopted me also. Once I agreed, then on the spur of the moment, they decided to adopt a boy too. Ida Kaminets suggested that they adopt Michael. But they were interested mainly in Deborah. It never really bothered me, but I think it hurt Michael a lot. You know, Robert, every time you suggest we make a trip to Europe I say I'm not interested. That's because I have no curiosity about Europe. Not the faintest. You hear older people who came from Europe say they want to go back, one last time, to look for the cobblestone streets of their childhood. I'm not curious. I had no childhood that I can remember. My life began the day I came to America. I put everything out of my mind before that. I'm living now, not then. The then is gone. My roots are here with you, with our children, with Deborah and Michael and even Sidney. My real parents, whoever they were, gave up their lives so that I would live. Leon and Rose adopted me and I cling to the feeling it was in memory of my real parents that I was adopted. Did Leon and Rose love Deborah and Michael and me? Probably not. Does it matter? They gave us everything they possessed because that was the only way they could show their feelings. But they protected us and cared for us and really loved their grandchildren as their own flesh and blood. And so time caught up. Deborah didn't know until today about Mrs. Safire's child; I told her."

"When did you find out?" Robert asked.

"Just a week before Mother went on that last trip to the Mountainview Hotel, where she died. She asked me to spend the afternoon with her. I thought it was for shopping for the trip. But we drove out to Beth David Hospital. In the children's wing at the hospital, in the board room, she showed me an oil painting of a child. I swear, Robert, the painting could have been of Deborah when she was twelve. She told me that it was painted a little while before the child died, that she was adopted from Mrs. Safire and all the rest, about how they hadn't originally planned to adopt Michael and me. She made me promise that I would never tell Deborah or Michael while she and Father were alive. I was free to tell them any time after their death. I waited two years."

"Did you tell Michael?"

"No," she replied.

"Will you?"

"I don't think so. He probably knows anyhow. Now that Deborah knows, I'd rather that she tell him."

"I wonder why your Mother told you all that?"

"She told me why. She said that she was afraid someday ghosts of the past would try to destroy her family and that the only protection against it would be emptying her heart of the secret she carried there for almost forty years."

Robert smiled at her, an appreciative smile.

"Does it bother you," he said, "that you were a piggyback deal, a tag-along?"

"No," she replied, "it's as if it never happened at all."

Chapter 20

THE REDEMPTION

Nothing's happened, everything's happened. Lots of blood, hunks of flesh, a dissecting table three thousand miles wide.

The three brothers-in-law left the dining room and entered Robert's library. All the furnishings had been Leon's and even the arrangement preserved the feeling of Leon's library. Rich leather trimmings and chairs. The photographs on the wall that had been signed by political celebrities with cordial greetings to Leon were arranged in exactly the same way they had been left in the apartment two floors below where Leon and Rose had lived for more than twenty years. From the children's room they could hear the laughter of young voices and their mother's gentle reproaches to quiet down and listen to the stories being read.

Robert turned the TV on to the news. Bombs, helicopters, litter bearers, a miner's strike, a racially tense situation in the South where a teenager had been shot in the back, the national guard placed on alert, street clashes between Negroes and police in New Jersey, reports of sniper fire and looting, tear gas.

"If things go on this way," Robert said, "this time next year there may be an all-out civil war."

"If more of them were willing to work and get off welfare, there wouldn't be so much noise," Sidney commented. "Do you know how goddamn hard it is to get a sleep-in maid?"

Michael imagined himself on the screen in place of the newscaster, making an appeal to Fay to return to him. He smiled at the idea. "You're the one," he said, looking at Robert, "who's convinced that Nixon is going to stop all the trouble, including inflation."

Bomb threats at federal office buildings, a threatened strike by cabdrivers, a suicide by a prisoner branded as official murder, an unidentified nude body of a woman in an abandoned car on the East Side, students setting fire to their dormitory in protest against a marijuana raid by police.

"Hey!" Sidney exclaimed, doubling up with forced laughter. "Look at that. That's what we're coming to!"

The newscaster's voice: "It may have been winter today for most of us, but for at least one man it was summer and a return to nature." The view was of Times Square. The jerky motion of a camera followed the slow pace of an elderly man walking completely naked through the noonday crowds of Times Square.

The newscaster's voice: "Apparently even nudity on the city streets doesn't phase our highly sophisticated citizenry. Notice the passers-by! A quick glance and they walk on as if this is usual, the everyday sight, at the city's busiest intersection."

The old, stooped man walked slowly along the street, people mechanically making way for him to pass, the view only of the rear of his body, his nude buttocks sagging. A jovial policeman approached, removing his coat. He pressed the man against the window of a coffee shop, wrapping him in the long blue coat. The old man's head turns to the camera; the face momentarily fills the screen.

"My god!" Michael gasps, leaping from the chair.

Sidney and Robert jumped from their seats and rushed to his side. Michael's face was covered with sweat, his arms trembling.

"Your heart?" Robert asked.

"What is it, Mike?"

"Shall we get a doctor?"

Michael shook his head. "It's . . . it's Dr. Mowiss."

The newscaster's face is filled with a toothy smile: "Nature boy of the year has been taken to Bellevue Hospital for observation."

"I'm leaving," Michael said. "I'm sorry to break up the party. Tell the girls good night for me."

"I'll go with you." Robert's tone was insistent.

"Who's Dr. Mowiss?" Sidney asks, without returning to the chair to watch the sports news.

"No," Michael replied. "I'll be all right."

On the way to the front door Robert would have liked to provide Michael with legal advice, to caution him that the newspapers could have a field day if reporters associated the naked man in Times Square with Leon's will and Michael's exemption from military service. Jesus! He would have liked to tell Michael—play it close to the vest, everyone could suffocate with embarrassment. Newsmen are vultures. Remember what they did to Nixon in California.

A wrinkled porter was mopping the small waiting room. A bucket gave off a sickening odor of disinfectant. A woman sat with her legs crossed on a low bench closest to the door opening into the admitting room. She wore a woolen kerchief tightly tied around her head and large dark glasses. A newspaper reporter and photographer were milling in a corner, grunting their dissatisfaction, tossing cigarette butts into the streams of slop that spilled over from the bucket.

Michael entered the waiting room, inadvertently making tracks where the floor had been mopped. The porter frowned at him.

The reporters approached him.

"You here for nature boy?"

"Are you?" he said.

"Yeah. We're doing a follow-up to the TV thing. It's too late for the morning editions, but it would make a kinda nice downbeat piece for a Saturday story. Are you a relative of nature boy's?"

"No," Michael answered. "A friend."

Their eyes bulged hungrily.

"I have a few questions," the reporter exclaimed.

"Have you had dinner?" Michael asked as he reached into his pocket.

"What's on your mind, mister?"

He tucked six twenty-dollar bills into the outside breast pocket of the reporter. The photographer looked on with relish.

"Why don't you two have a good dinner and some nice wine on me?"

The photographer grinned at his associate, eagerly nodding his head.

"Forget nature boy?"

"Yes," Michael said softly. "Forget him."

"Well, it was a meatball piece, anyway." The two of them began to leave. The reporter turned. "Is he some kind of rich nut? He had no identification on him."

The photographer poked his arm. "Come on. He was stark naked, how could he have identification? Let's go."

"He's circumcized. That's something," the reporter persisted as his companion nudged him toward the exit.

Michael walked to the admitting-room door and shook the handle. Locked. He had not noticed the woman sitting on the bench.

She stood up, her hand slowly lifting toward him.

"Fay!" He threw his face against her, knocking the dark glasses to the floor. His arms locked her in his embrace.

The door opened. A haggard man in a white jacket stood in the opening, a stethoscope hanging about his neck. He coughed to attract their attention.

"I'm the attending psychiatrist. You're the young woman who asked to see me?"

Except for their hands which remained clutched, they moved apart.

"Yes," she said anxiously.

"This gentleman?"

"A friend."

"It's not good news," the doctor said. "He's had a severe cerebrovascular episode. In short, a stroke. It's not the first; apparently he's been here before with the same symptoms. Bad prognosis. Full paralysis on the left side, constriction, and breathing is touch and go. Extensive brain damage. Signs of accelerating cardiac insufficiency.

Occasional fibrillation. What else can I say? He's an old cuss, late seventies I'd guess, and hasn't been in even reasonable health for years."

"How long?"

The doctor shrugged. "It could be a matter of minutes. A day or two at the most.

"Technically"—he paused and fingered the buttons on the white jacket—"he's still under police jurisdiction. But, what the hell, it won't make any difference. Come on."

In the furthest corner of the ward, where the only sounds were incoherent gurglings, a nurse was daubing a needle with alcohol.

"Sedation," the doctor whispered. "The only thing we can do at this point."

"Can he be moved?" Michael asked.

"A private hospital or home? That what you have in mind?"

"Yes."

"It's a waste of money. Here, it's free, unless a caseworker finds he has assets."

"None."

"Then why waste your money? Better to help those who can get some meaningful benefit. Care for the living." He turned the lamp so that Mowiss's face became visible.

"The nurse will let you out. I've got some paperwork, more red tape. I'll be on duty until seven. Call me if you think I can do something." He scratched a number on a prescription sheet and handed it to Michael.

Michael reached into his pocket.

"No need," said the psychiatrist with a wave of his hand. "Give something to the porter if you want. The poor bastard is a widower supporting eight children."

The face seemed shrunken, the mouth open and gasping for air, the eyes shut tight as if wishing not to see.

They held hands at Mowiss's bedside without looking at one another. It was less than twelve hours from the time Michael had last seen him, but the blanched face looked different, the features altered, the slight, remaining animation controlled by dark forces. He was, in effect, already in a different world.

He looked at the thin, cracked lips that would not speak

again. Mishka, Mishka, little chum, he wanted the lips to say. He heard only a coarse, rasping, gargling stream of breath.

"Here!" Leaning to one side so as not to jostle and wake the child, he reached into the pocket of his coat, removed five silvery coins, tossed them onto the muddy ground, and buried them with a grinding of the heel of his boot. "A deal's a deal. Live, you little son of a bitch."

He was high over the man's head, smothered with manly kisses, far away on a sun-filled green field in France. It was a falsehood, the face only wore a grotesque mask, he was again pretending, taking one of the innumerable disguises, pretenses, changes of character he had played out since his first visit during another age.

Mowiss's dirty gray, matted hair was twisted into two small pointed tufts on either side of his head. They were like the budding horns of a young ram. The thin lips closed over the teeth with a hissing sound. For a moment, the eyes opened, stared into the blankness of the hospital room and shut. Sleep. The sedation had gone into effect. The body under the sheet seemed to stretch. The lips turned into a defiant snarl.

A nurse passed. She smiled at the man and woman standing silently, their hands interwoven, and noticed the strange angle of the pale head on the pillow in the full light of the lamp. She approached, pulled the eyelids apart with a thumb and forefinger, and, placing the bulb of her stethoscope to the man's chest, said softly: "I'm sorry. He's just expired."

Silently Michael and Fay returned to the brownstone building on Ninety-Third Street, where she had not been for a year and a half. Nothing had been changed. They undressed and went to bed, seeking each other desperately and lovingly in the darkness.

One of them held the littlest child of them all, frail, still undernourished in spite of adequate food, strangely silent except when in pain. This was the illegal male that had been rejected by the dogs.

"What shall we call him?" said one of the women of the kindergarten.

"Abelard," her companion replied, laughing.

184

"Why that?"

"It's a name from a love story."

"They would have a fit if we called him that. No. Another."

"The rules say the name should begin with the letter of the month. M. It's got to be M."

They rose early and after breakfast walked to a funeral home a few blocks away. The home made all the arrangements including a burial plot in a nonsectarian cemetery in Westchester, about fifteen miles north of the city. Some snowflakes fell, the first of the winter. Except for the chauffeur of the car provided by the funeral home and the hearse driver, they were the only ones to watch the wooden coffin lowered into the freshly dug grave. At Michael's request Robert sent a cablegram to Rosalia in care of the American Consul in Milan. It was a short message, no reply expected.

Michael and Fay each tossed a handful of earth atop the coffin and Fay arranged a bouquet of forget-me-nots on the mound of earth at the edges of the grave.

In the limousine, Michael said, "Fay, I love you so much."

"I'll never leave you, Michael. I love you with all my heart."

Chapter 21

THE CHANUKAH PARTY

The arbitrary date chosen for Naomi's birthday coincided with the ancient Jewish Festival of Lights, a celebration of defiance, liberation, joy, and it brought Deborah and Sidney out of their country seclusion. Freshly cut from their greenhouse, Sidney brought thirty-one very long-stemmed American Beauty roses; the same number of candles on the pink birthday cake that Deborah had baked. Their baby son, Leon, only a few months old, slept quietly in Cassie's room and whenever she was not serving hors d'oeuvres or the dinner, she looked in at the infant. Their eight-year-old daughter played in the game room with Naomi's three children. Cassie made an exaggerated gesture of shuddering when they raced through the dining room shouting and laughing.

Judge Lieberg dropped in to congratulate Naomi. In spite of a magisterial mane of white hair and carefully shaven cheeks he seemed to be shrinking. He was three years away from his eightieth birthday. He handed Naomi a blue velvet-covered box from Cartier and kissed her fondly on the forehead. "Open it later," he told her. "When you open the other gifts." He took a glass of champagne and toasted her health. "To you, my dear Naomi, a good life, a long life." He chatted amiably with Michael, Robert, and Sidney, then left, holding Cassie's hand as she led him to the door.

Deborah and Sidney refused to take part in business discussions regarding the estate. The hundreds of letters that poured in from all over the country each week requesting donations and contributions were turned over to Robert's secretary for reply. Whenever documents regarding the will had to be signed, an attorney from Judge Lieberg's office hand-delivered them to their country place with a brief note from the judge saying that Naomi had approved. It mattered little to either Deborah or Sidney that the will was being contested and that more than a year and a half had dragged by and matters still weren't resolved. Whatever reasons Michael, Robert, and Naomi had for resisting a settlement were of small concern to them. They refused to hear about it, refused to discuss the matter. While the pregancy and birth of little Leon were painful because of the emotional and physical complications of the miscarriage three years earlier, Deborah had succeeded in losing a great deal of weight and life in the country with Sidney amidst the year-round greenhouse flowers was calm, comfortable, and happy. When Robert gushed enthusiastically about the dinner invitation with a Nobel Prize-winning physician, suggesting an endowment for a nuclear biology research center that would probe the mysteries of existence, Deborah and Sidney looked at him blankly. They preferred to talk about subjects the children were learning in school.

At one point Judge Lieberg sent a legal paper and a request for their signatures agreeing that they would undertake no new programs or benefactions, other than those initiated by Leon and Rose, until they each came into their full inheritance at age thirty-two. Signing the agreement was an enormous relief; at least for a while, Robert would not be tempted to "talk business."

Out of respect for each other's moods, the Chanukah party dinner, like most of their family gatherings since Leon and Rose died, was limited to animated conversation about their children, except for Michael who seemed to be listening politely but said little. Robert refrained from talking about his recent, intense interest and participation in Republican Party matters. A year before Sidney had said, and Deborah had nodded eager approval, that all political activity, hence all politicians, were corrupt and that if people minded their own business the world would be better off. Robert would have liked to tell them he was rather proud that his home had become a regular meeting place for moderate young Republicans like himself and that they expected to wield much influence in the selection of the Republican presidential candidate for 1968, that it was virtually assured that with a Republican victory, he would be offered and would probably accept a sub-cabinet position with a new administration.

When these meetings took place, Naomi led the women to the living room as the men followed Robert to the library, and she discussed plans for organizing a drive for better participation of women in Republican state committees. From time to time Michael joined the sessions in the library and made pledges of token amounts whenever the group appeared to take an affirmative position on defending the rights of antiwar dissenters. More often than not he attended meetings in a Riverside Drive apartment house where Reform Democrats spoke vitriolically against the war policies of President Johnson, railed against the war in Vietnam, and sought funds for legal-defense committees for college radicals, antiwar candidates, and what was referred to as the "movement." He pledged ten times more money to these groups than to the ones meeting in Robert's apartment.

"Dahlias!" exclaimed Naomi with a bemused smile.

"I'm entering my dahlias in the annual show of the Westchester Horticultural Society. Sidney is crazy about them. He even found a special way of fertilizing them when they're still tiny and in flats."

"Flats?" her sister inquired.

Deborah explained. Robert listened with insincere attention. Michael watched the flickering of candle flames in the ornate golden candelabra.

No one mentioned the piece in the *Wall Street Journal* about Sidney that referred to him as "an outstanding example of that new breed of dynamic millionaire under thirty-five." It told about Sidney's reluctance to be interviewed, his aloofness to publicity, and the "daring investment concepts" he had put into action. Robert yearned to lure him into the library to discuss deals they could jointly undertake; after all, Leon's estate would be a powerful financial lever in any enterprise. His gestures to Sidney went unheeded and whatever he knew about Sidney's burgeoning business empire he learned about in the financial press. He never brought up business in the family circle. There was envy, too, in Robert's intense desire to involve Sidney in a joint venture. Leon's properties and wealth had slowly accumulated over a period of forty years, Sidney's in less than two. Much of Leon's equity over which he had nominal control was tied up in land and buildings, and unlike Sidney's money, according to the *Journal*, the amount of risk capital available was quite modest. He envied Sidney's apparent ability to multiply his interests by a few phone calls from his country place as compared to the tremendous legwork he had to undertake in consummating land deals that often fell through. Trying to devise schemes he could propose to his brother-in-law for mutual financial benefit became a major preoccupation when he was not exhorting Michael to settle Mowiss's contest of the will.

Michael and Robert saw each other every day of the week, for the two of them jointly managed the realty interests Leon had built up.

The senior employees of the firm respected Robert's legal acumen, his shrewdness in detecting what could be fatal flaws in a contract, a flair bordering on brilliance in countering proposals to provide the most advantageous tax loopholes for the company. But they looked to Michael for perceptiveness of opportunities; they often declared that Michael had inherited his father's hard bargaining qualities and fiery enthusiasm in pursuing deals both sound and profitable. Without formal training in either architecture or engineering, Michael had the uncanny ability of scanning blueprints and knowing precisely at what points subcontractors were prepared to cut corners. He could and did outwit the chiselers at their own game; he could tell from the way traffic moved at one of the construction sites when police were looking for a payoff to prevent delays, and knew which staff member to assign to the delicate task of approaching which police officials with appropriate "gifts." Robert excelled in dealing with bankers and investors. The older members of the firm, although anxious in the months that followed Leon's death about whether the two young men would wreck the company, had come to appreciate the ways the son and son-in-law complemented one another and felt completely secure that the firm would continue to prosper and grow under their youthful leadership.

The two got along cordially and worked successfully together as long as two topics were not broached by Robert; one was the contest by Dr. Mowiss and the other was Fay Buttonwood.

After Naomi handed out portions of the pink birthday cake she opened the gifts. The children asked their mothers to accompany them to the playroom, where they kneeled on the floor and amid laughter began spinning colorful tops decorated with Hebrew letters. A childish gambling game began with gold foil-covered chocolates awarded to the winners. Deborah delighted the children with slight of hand, making the chocolate coins vanish in front of their eyes. "Again! Again!" they cried, and she obliged.

"Are you going skiing this winter, Sid?" Robert asked.

"No, I don't care for it. It's too much trouble. You freeze your nuts waiting for the tow. We may take a cruise. Debbie's never been to St. Croix. How about you?"

The men discussed possible winter vacations.

With the estate settled, Robert's spirits soared. He and Michael played tennis every day at noon on the court they had decided to build atop their office building. They succeeded in persuading Sidney to join them, at first once and then several times a week. Tennis developed into a passion for Sidney and he had a court built as an addition to his country house. Little by little, tennis games among them on weekdays in the city and on weekends at Sidney's and Deborah's place gradually won Sidney over to the idea of joint business ventures. The articles in the *Wall Street Journal* began to speak about the "troika," the three brothers-in-law who were creating an impressive track record in every one of their ventures. As their business undertakings flourished, the three decided to make regular contributions to political activities. Michael limited his interests to Democratic Party matters, Robert to the Republican Party, but Sidney gave to both simultaneously.

As Naomi and Deborah spent more time together, genuinely happy that the three brothers-in-law were getting along amicably on both personal and business matters, Naomi was able to involve her sister in many of the decisions that had to be made regarding the benefactions, old and new, that had to be made consistent with the terms of Leon's will. As the day of their thirty-second birthdays approached, Deborah's coming a month before Naomi's, they began to plan the creation of a philanthropic foundation that would gradually assume responsibility for Leon's donations and shape a program that reflected their own personal interests, whatever these turned out to be. On their thirty-second birthdates, each would receive the full share of the estate left by Leon. They had no specific plans, other than to make provision for Ida Kaminets to continue the work that in spite of her advancing years and failing health she refused to curtail.

Fay shared in their weekend life as well as in their social and theater life in the city. She was accepted by them and loved as one would love a close friend or sister. No mention was ever made of the fact that Fay and Michael were not married, although they lived together, or that neither Fay nor Michael ever broached the question of marriage. When Fay and Michael visited the country place on weekends, they were given a large sunny guest room on the ground floor that had a terrace from which one could see the silver, serpentine band of the Hudson River. The children called her Aunt Fay and she was affectionate and playful with them. In the summer of 1968, a few months before Naomi and Deborah were to become fabulously wealthy in their own right, and still five years away from the date of Michael's full inheritance, the first swellings of Fay's belly, showing the unmistakable signs of pregnancy, still did not produce discussions of marriage. Instead, the three women sat in the shade and watched Michael, Robert, and Sidney play with the children.

Sidney ran to where they were. He was laughing and breathless. He threw himself into the grass at their feet.

"Whew! The kids are rough!" he exclaimed. "Hey, you know, I threw my hat in the ring. I'm in politics. I filed a petition to run for election to the town school board. I want to make sure that little Leon will get a decent education. And the yokels are already carrying on. Word is making the rounds about the rich, Jewish carpetbagger from the city. They'll probably even come up with something about my brother-in-law Michael living in sin with a beautiful pregnant blonde."

Deborah and Naomi both flashed an embarrassed, scolding look at him. Fay blushed and smiled at the same time.

"Whoops! I said something wrong."

"Why don't you go inside and take a shower, Sidney?" Deborah asked. He left them, tripping on his heels in a mock, sulking gait.